MARGARET WAY
Outback Surrender

D0500788

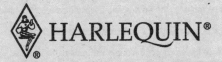

HARLEQUIN®

TORONTO • NEW YORK • LONDON
AMSTERDAM • PARIS • SYDNEY • HAMBURG
STOCKHOLM • ATHENS • TOKYO • MILAN • MADRID
PRAGUE • WARSAW • BUDAPEST • AUCKLAND

ISBN 0-373-03775-9

OUTBACK SURRENDER

First North American Publication 2003.

This edition published by arrangement with Harlequin Books S.A.

® and TM are trademarks of the publisher. Trademarks indicated with ® are registered in the United States Patent and Trademark Office, the Canadian Trade Marks Office and in other countries.

Visit us at www.eHarlequin.com

Printed in U.S.A.

CHAPTER ONE

SHELLEY hit the pavement with a fast light step that belied her tiredness. It was late Friday afternoon and she'd all but completed her list of "must-dos" in the town of Koomera Crossing. Her first meeting, with the bank manager, hadn't gone too badly, but the meeting with her father's solicitor— the only one in the town—had not been so good. She'd then ordered fresh food supplies from the general store, where they always did a marvellous job. That had been the most important and most pressing need. Supplies had to be ordered in to accommodate a small party of Japanese guests due in a month's time. Those supplies would be airfreighted out to the station before the tourists' arrival.

She'd stocked up on all the non-perishable items, and now she was going to buy a few little treats for herself, just to keep her spirits up. Toiletries, mainly. Soaps, shampoos, creams, a bit of make-up and the like. Usually she spent very little on herself, only peanuts on clothes and cosmetics, but she made sure she looked after her hair and skin. Those precious assets had to last her a lifetime, after all.

She was dog-tired even for a girl with plenty of go, and she had to force her legs to see out the distance. She'd started out from home, Wybourne Station, in the pre-dawn, making a fairly quick trip—some three hours over rough Outback roads—before she hit Koomera Crossing, the nearest thing to civilisation in this part of the world.

South-West Queensland really was the Back O'Beyond, but she loved her desert home with a passion. Nowhere else could offer her such peace and freedom, such vast open spaces. This was the Timeless Land, sacred to all aborigines. Shelley too revelled in her extraordinary environment—the living desert, with its vivid pottery colours, undulating red sands and surreal rock monuments. There was nowhere quite like the Outback for mystique. Its very antiquity gripped the soul.

It also kept her close to Sean, her guardian angel, her twin brother. Sean had drowned when they were six. Even now she remembered the sound of his sweet voice calling to her as she'd run madcap in the homestead's rambling, overgrown garden...

Shel...Shel...Shel...

Sean had always run to her, his twin, for love, for reassurance and comfort, rather than to their older sister, Amanda, or even their mother. And even after the terrible day of the accident, of which Shelley had no clear recollection but of chaos and high, screaming voices, Sean had still accompanied her on her childhood adventures. Hadn't he woken her every dawn of her life, patting her forehead and pulling her ear? "Wake up, Shel. The sun'll burn a hole in you."

Sean! Always destined to remain a beautiful little boy, Titian curls his halo, rosebud lips moving soundlessly, his eyes like shining jewels, a gauzy white radiance all around him.

That was what twins were like. They shared a bond that meant they were never parted, not even in death. Still, heartbreak was never far from Shelley. Her memories of her little brother were bittersweet, but the power and magic of their love for each other sustained her even now.

She walked on briskly, calling a pleasantry here and there. Nearly everyone in the town was as well known to her as she was to them.

She had no intention of returning to Wybourne tonight. She couldn't possibly find the strength for the long drive after hoofing around the town for hours, always trying to find shelter under awnings from the dry, burning sun.

It was the greatest mystery to her and to everyone else— and sometimes she thought her older sister Amanda was secretly outraged by the fact—but she didn't have a single freckle. She the redhead with the untameable firewheel mop. Her skin was often referred to as "porcelain". She had to thank her darling now deceased maternal grandmother Moira, born in County Kerry, Ireland, for that. Ditto the rose-gold mane, the green eyes and, it had to be said, the Irish temper when aroused.

She was staying at the town's only pub, run by Mick Donovan. The food was fine and the accommodation was comfortable and spotlessly clean. She couldn't wait to run a bubble bath—what a luxury—and just soak. But first she'd have to buy the bubbles.

She was standing in the town's pharmacy, deciding between two—jasmine-scented or gardenia—when a hand tweaked one of her curls. And not all that gently, she thought in surprise. She was sure in the course of the day she'd spoken to just about everyone who was out and about in town. Station born and bred, she'd been coming into Koomera Crossing all her life.

She was so quick on her feet she caught the telltale trace of devilry on a handsome mouth.

Excitement welled up so fast it made her dizzy. There stood Brock Tyson, right there in the flesh. His bearing held the same fiery male pride, the same high-mettled look that put her in mind of a powerful plunging stallion. As a full-grown man he was magnificent, but the dark brooding hadn't died in him. She sensed it plainly as she faced him. The town, indeed the entire Outback, hadn't seen or heard of him in years, though he was one of their own.

Daniel Brockway Tyson had been one of the wildest and most daring young men the vast South-West had ever known. Brock had found all sorts of marvellous ways of living on the edge. Sometimes as a boy he would go off into the desert for days, giving no account of his adventures when he finally got home to Mulgaree, where he had been met by the predictable whipping. Mulgaree was the flagship of the Kingsley chain of cattle stations. Old man Kingsley,

Brock's grandfather, ran it like a private fiefdom. It was he who had administered the whipping, but he'd never broken Brock's spirit.

"Why, if it isn't sweet little Shelley Logan," Brock exclaimed, his remarkable light eyes moving over her. "You haven't changed at all."

"I certainly have!" She allowed him to steer her out of the aisle. "All it takes is time."

"Give me a minute and it'll become more apparent." He grinned, continuing his inspection. "How are you?"

Shelley Logan had been just a kid when he'd left. So pretty, so innocent, so bruised by fate. Brock hadn't forgotten the enchanting little Logan twins and their tragedy. There wouldn't be a soul for thousands of miles around who wasn't familiar with the sad story of how little Sean Logan had lost his life.

"I'm fine, Brock." Shelley was completely unprepared for the onrush of surprise and delight. "Where in the world did you spring from? I've been in town all day, yet not a single soul mentioned you were back, let alone right here in Koomera Crossing."

His features, which might have been chiselled by a master sculptor, tightened. "It was not my idea but my beloved grandfather's. It seems he can no longer endure our estrangement. Can you beat that? He kicked me out almost five years ago to the day; now he relays such an impassioned plea I simply couldn't turn him down."

"He's ill?" The thought sprang immediately to her mind. "People start thinking of family reconciliations at those times."

"He's dying in the way of mere mortals," Brock told her caustically. "Of course he never thought he was one. I'm not letting any cat out of the bag; it'll only take a day for it to be all over town."

Shelley looked up at him. She had to tilt her head back. Brock was easily six-three. She was vertically challenged at five-two. "I don't know what to say, Brock. I always thought your grandfather was very cruel to you." The whole Outback was in agreement on that.

"Sure he was," he said carelessly. "But I used to get my own back. I had the rare pleasure of telling him off. Not so my poor mother."

"How is she?" Shelley asked, eager for news.

He glanced beyond her, out into the mirage-stalked street, his finely cut nostrils flaring. The look in his eyes was very complex and disturbing. "She didn't come home with me, Shel. I buried her in Ireland—the land of her ancestors. She was taken by cancer."

"Brock!" Tender-hearted Shelley found her eyes stinging. "I am so sorry. I know how close you were to your mother. And she to you." Shaken, she took a deep breath of air.

"So I'm alone in the world," he said simply. "My dad simply vanished like a puff of smoke when I was six, and I can't count the rest of my family as family. They're more sworn enemies—or plotters at the very least. Cousin Philip and his mother, dear Frances. She's always hated me."

Shelley's expression clouded. "Deep down I swear she admires you."

"Really? I've never heard it." His eyes, a lovely lustrous silver, such a foil for his dark colouring, strayed over her.

She felt her whole body flush. Brock Tyson's sex appeal was enormous. Once she'd had the mother of all crushes on him—he a charismatic, experienced twenty-one to her virginal sixteen. He'd even kissed her once. Not that he would ever remember. It had been at a bush dance. Her first. He'd swooped on her in an excess of high spirits, flirting, reckless, whirling her off her feet with a whoop of laughter. She'd never forgotten the hardly-to-be-borne excitement of her first kiss—hitherto unsurpassed, worst luck! Brock had always loved the girls, and they'd all loved him.

"In some ways you were Philip's hero," she mused. "He longed to be like you. Brave and daring. Unafraid of your grandfather. You two cousins should have been great friends.''

''That was impossible, Shelley.'' He shook his black head. ''Kingsley and dear Aunt Frances set us head to head. Who was to be the heir? The one who challenged or the one who toed the line? Is Phil still sweet on you?'' He said it suddenly, as though he didn't much like the idea.

''Relax, we're only friends. We've known one another forever. My parents approve of him, which is kind of a plus. It's wonderful to see you, Brock. I'm terribly, terribly glad you're back again.''

He smiled down at her, clearly amused by her obvious pleasure and sincerity. ''You always were a sweet little thing.'' Looking at her wide, sensitive mouth, he had an unexpected flash of memory. ''I seem to remember kissing you once. Did I?''

''It was normal for you to kiss all the girls,'' she said drolly.

''I don't recall kissing your sister. Is she married yet?''

''No. And how do you know I'm not?'' She tilted a brow in mock indignation.

''You still look like a rosebud.'' He gave that lazily sexy smile. ''People tell me you're running some sort of tourist venture out at Wybourne?''

''I am, and I'm very proud of it.'' Her tone was calm and self-assured, belying her girlish appearance. ''It's taken time, but we're getting off the ground. A lot of the planning has fallen on me. My poor parents never did recover from Sean's death. It's left them rather tired of life.''

''I know what it's like to mourn. I bet Amanda is a big help to you,'' Brock said with a touch of sarcasm, remembering all too clearly Shelley's pretty, highly flirtatious and self-centred sister.

''Couldn't do without her,'' Shelley said loyally, Martha to Amanda's Mary and so well used to it, it had become second nature. ''Amanda shines where I don't.''

''Where might that be?'' he asked sceptically.

"She plays the piano and she has an attractive singing voice. Country and western—that sort of thing. Guests like it. Plus she's very pretty, as I'm sure you'll remember."

"And you're not?" He upped the excitement with a lingering gaze.

"Stop flattering me, Brock Tyson," she said mock severely. "I don't know how to deal with it."

"I bet you do. In fact, you've acquired so much poise you might be getting on for middle-aged," he joked. "How on earth do you manage to keep the freckles at bay?"

Sex appeal simply oozed out of this man. With those eyes of his on her Shelley felt like splashing herself with cold water. "I can't take the credit, Brock. Just genes, I suppose. How long are you going to stay with us?"

"As long as I can tolerate it," he said, all of a sudden moody, but still so charismatic he took her breath away. "Kingsley, about to face his Maker, thinks it's time to get a few things straightened out. My mother was his only daughter. He was supposed to have adored her. That was before my father came along to claim her heart. I never saw any sign of love or affection from my grandfather towards my mother. He just found ways to upset and humiliate her. And hey, Shel, it's not all his money: Grandma Brockway brought a fortune to the marriage. It was Brockway money that kept my mother and me in the beginning. After that I was able to pay our way. Kingsley sent us off penniless. As you say, he was a cruel man. It's just that I found his cruelty easier to endure than my poor mother."

"Surely in asking you to return home he's begging your forgiveness?" she suggested, feeling the bitterness and anger coming off him in waves.

"Then he's going to be disappointed," he clipped off. "Judgement Day is coming for Rex Kingsley."

"Pray God he accepts it," she said quietly. "What did you do all the time you were away?" Rex Kingsley had never mentioned his daughter or his grandson from the day they left.

"Work." He shrugged. "I had to, as we were pretty much broke. I've been involved in breeding and training racehorses at a top stud in Ireland. Impossible to imagine a place more different to our Outback!"

"Ireland!" she echoed. "So that's where you got to! So far away. I often wonder what our ancestors thought of their strange new land. Ireland. How exciting! I'm going to go one day. That's a promise I've made to myself. You always were marvellous at handling horses, Brock. You've even developed an Irish lilt. Did you like it?"

"Loved it." His silver eyes sparkled. "You know how us outbackers are with horses. The Irish are the same. The instant rapport paid off. I did a good job. I made good money, and earned respect from people I admired. I kept my mother secure until she died."

"No one here knew where you went."

"Kingsley cut us off completely. I returned the favour. More than anything I blame him for turning his back on my mother. Why would I want to notify him when she died?"

"I'm surprised you came home," she ventured. Brock, always vivid, had developed a very commanding not to say daunting presence mixed in with the familiar charm.

"Just occasionally I remember I'm a Kingsley on my mother's side. If dear old Grandpa wants to reinstate me in his will—and he seems to want to—I'm not going to stop him. My mother was owed. I'm owed." The silver eyes took on a hard glitter. "They call it atonement."

"So you're staying at Mulgaree? That can't be easy." She remembered how Philip and Frances had always been so jealous of Brock, with his energy and effortless skills, the way he stood up to his domineering grandfather.

"It's not as though I have to see anyone if I don't want to." He gave a brief laugh. "Heaven knows the old barn is big enough."

"You used to love it," she reminded him dryly.

"And I still do, Emerald Eyes."

Shelley Logan was no longer the cute little teenager he remembered. She'd matured. She had a woman's sensitivity and perception and she wasn't afraid to speak her mind. Back then she'd been way too young for him, but in the interim the rosebud had opened up velvety perfumed petals.

He continued to stare at her, holding her gaze captive. Despite the poise he hadn't been prepared for, she was flushed with colour. Her wild red-gold hair lay loose around her shoulders. Her beautiful eyes were large and lustrous, her mouth sensitive and her chin prettily pointed. If it wouldn't jeopardize their old easy friendship he would have told her she looked damned sexy.

"So what's the verdict?" she asked dryly, with a tilt of her chin.

"Just checking," he drawled. "All right, Shel. You've changed. You've grown up. So what are you doing right now? On your way home to your family?" He recalled the bleakness of Wybourne, the Logans' loss of all joy.

"Tomorrow. I can't make the return trip the same day."

"God, I would think not. Look at you! The wind could pick you up and blow you away. Still giving you hell, are they?" In his experience nothing really ever changed.

She shook her head, her tone mildly chastening. "You shouldn't talk like that, Brock. I love my family. We survive. I guess I'll always bear the pain for surviving when Sean didn't."

"You should have said blame. But it was a terrible accident, Shelley. You were a very young child when it happened."

"I know, but it doesn't seem to help." She looked away.

"Not when you're not allowed to forget. Hell," he burst out explosively, as though the small space couldn't contain him—as indeed it couldn't. "Let's get out of here." He'd been aware from the moment he'd greeted her that every head was turned in their direction, the well-oiled gossip machine getting underway.

"Where? I need to get something here." She glanced in the direction of the counter.

"Then do it," he ordered briskly. "You must be staying at the pub?"

"As it happens, I am." Brock was still pure flame. Which gave cautious old Shelley an excellent chance of getting burned.

"Then so am I. I was going to sleep in the truck, but Mick can sort me out a room. What do you say we have dinner? I see Koomera Crossing's redoubtable schoolmarm Harriet Crompton has opened up a restaurant. No doubt about Miss Crompton! She always was a woman of many talents."

"That would be lovely, Brock." After her earlier fatigue excitement had started to run at full throttle.

"We have lots to catch up on. The fact is Phil advised me—maybe it was a heavy warning—that you were his girl-friend?" Silver eyes emitted sparks.

"Why hasn't he told me that, then?" she said flippantly.

"You're too good for him, Shelley." Brock's antagonism towards his cousin spilled out.

She stared up at him for a moment before she answered. Even in misty green Ireland his skin must have seen plenty of sunshine. His olive skin was like polished bronze.

"Isn't that a little cruel? I feel sorry for Philip. Your grandfather is very hard on him, and his mother has such high expectations. Philip is under constant pressure to per-form. Not that your grandfather allows him any real re-sponsibility."

"Just keeps him on a tight leash. Must be hard for Phil. He was a dopey kid."

"Whereas you were as bad as you could get." She soft-ened the charge with a smile. "Philip, unfortunately, is still very much under the influence of his mother. Now, I'll pay for this, Brock, if you can wait." She settled hurriedly on the gardenia-scented bath gel.

"I think you're right." He gave the nod to her choice. "Gardenia goes with your beautiful skin."

*   *   *

Of course she didn't have a dress. She should have thought of that before. But Brock's off-the-cuff invitation to have dinner with him had chased all thought from her mind. For the first time since she'd attended the wedding of her friends Christine and Mitch Claydon she had a deep desire to look pretty.

How? She took another look at herself in the old-fashioned, slightly speckled pier mirror. It stood in a corner of the small room where fresh cotton sheets, pillowslips and towels smelled deliciously of boronia.

Trim and tidy. If called on that was the way Shelley would have described herself. Unlike her sister Amanda she had no wardrobe of pretty dresses. Her day-to-day dress was a practical work uniform—jeans and a cotton shirt. She stared at herself dreamily. Brock Tyson had always been kind to her, for all his dashing but undeniably moody nature. These days he looked like a man well able to handle himself in any situation. Tough. A bit like Rex Kingsley himself, who was as harsh and unyielding as the very terrain of his desert kingdom.

Finally she decided on a dash half a block away to the town's little dress shop, where she'd seen a very pretty blouse displayed in the window. The only reason she'd resisted it was that she had too few occasions to wear anything so frivolously pretty. Basic denim was her scene. This top was a kind of patchwork of yellow cotton and lace, with little ribbons and rosettes for a trim. The owner assured her it could be worn successfully with her white jeans.

Très chic! She'd have to take her word for it. At least she had some make-up and a fairly new pair of white leather trainers she'd brush up.

Shelley felt wildly excited, but tried to bring the whole thing back into focus. By taking her out tonight Brock was probably trying to ward off the tensions of being home. Besides, she'd always associated Brock Tyson with excitement and—it had to be said—danger. It seemed to swirl around him like smoke.

He was a young man who had sustained many psychological wounds, even if the scars from his physical beatings had healed. The assaults by his autocratic grandfather had stopped with one fist-to-fist bout when Brock was fifteen and already topping six feet. One of the station hands who had witnessed it, open-mouthed and secretly overjoyed, had told the story to a mate, who'd told it to another mate in the Koomera Crossing pub. The gossip had spread like wildfire and the whole town had known within twenty-four hours.

"Old bastard Kingsley took a beating! And about time. I tell ya, it was something to see!" This along with plenty of chortles that hadn't lasted long. The informer had been promptly sacked, finding it very difficult to get station work within a huge radius.

Brock had earned his badge of courage, but had shown that he had a dark side. It would pay Shelley to remember that now.

The last thing Brock had thought he would be doing this evening was socializing. Truth was, he'd been feeling incredibly bad since he'd buried his mother—as though her early death had been somehow his fault. He'd certainly given her plenty of grief by being always at loggerheads with his grandfather. Not that she had ever blamed him or breathed a word of it. But the wound would never heal; the grief would never be buried. He hated his grandfather, who had cast them off all alone. Hated him and wasn't about to beg God's forgiveness. Once he'd even accused his grandfather of getting rid of his own father, Rory, who supposedly had "run off like a cur", to disappear without trace. But men in the Outback went missing all the time.

Was that what happened to his father? Knowing his grandfather, he could see him shooting anyone who challenged his authority in cold blood. He was that type. A megalomaniac. Having so much power and money could do that to an already mean man. His grandfather had been en-

raged by his only daughter's runaway marriage. He had tried
to have the marriage annulled, but failed. His mother had
already been pregnant with him. God knew why his parents
had allowed Kingsley to dictate to them, bringing them back
to Mulgaree, where Brock had been born in an upstairs bedroom.

His father had stuck it out, enmity and harsh treatment
notwithstanding. All for his mother, who had felt too helpless to know what to do. But six years on Rory Tyson had
disappeared, leaving a note his grandfather had burned after
showing it to Koomera Crossing's police constable, who had
been sent to investigate the disappearance.

After that—nothing. And there had been no news from
Rory for all these years. Brock had investigated but drawn
nothing but blanks trying to trace his father. He would get
square with his grandfather for that. Getting square was important.

With a muffled oath Brock fought out of the bleak
thoughts that threatened to swallow him up. He turned back
to the task of getting dressed. His black hair was still damp
from the shower, but already drying in the heat. He felt it
was too curly, too long, though women always told him how
much they liked it. In his experience women were always
ready to say something nice. Men were the bastards.

Swiftly he pulled on a clean shirt. Lucky he had it with
him. What the hell was he doing? These days he wanted to
be by himself, to lick his wounds. So why a night out in
town? The thing was he'd always found something endear-
ing about the little Logan girl, who had grown into quite a
woman. Her twin, Sean, had been the image of her. The
drowning had been a terrible tragedy that had left the boy's
parents half mad; the sadness had affected the entire town
and the outlying stations. The mother, it was said, still lay
in bed crying all day, and the father, Paddy Logan, had
allowed no one to forget that tragic day. Least of all his
younger daughter.

They had been beautiful little creatures, those Logan

twins. Everyone had thought it wonderful the way Shelley looked after Sean like a little mother. It wasn't right the way she'd been treated since his death. She'd taken far too much punishment from her family. Like Brock had. It created a bond between them. Come to that, he hadn't really forgotten kissing her at some dance. She'd been no more than sixteen but it had stuck in his memory, like a tune. He had a feeling that Shelley Logan with her lovely smile, on the outside so calm and collected, was bottling up a lot of passion. She was a redhead, after all. Red was nature's fire sign.

But what sort of a person was her sister, Amanda? Sitting at the piano playing and singing while Shelley was probably toiling away in the kitchen, preparing a meal for her parties of tourists. He doubted if she'd get much help from her poor mother. The few people in town he'd spoken to about the Logans had assured him things were as bad as ever for the family—except for Shelley's new venture, which had taken off. Everyone admired her. Shelley Logan was a capable, hard-working young woman with plenty of guts. That was the word according to Koomera Crossing.

All Brock knew was that sweet little female creatures like Shelley Logan eased a man's soul. And Lord knew how he thirsted for some area of peace. But romance wasn't on the agenda for him. Not even a brief affair. Certainly not with the girl he'd watched grow up. He couldn't plan anything. Not with his future so undecided.

He knew he wouldn't find peace at Mulgaree. But fronting up to his grandfather was a fierce necessity. Mulgaree was where he had been born, and his mother and his uncle Aaron, Philip's father, before him. Philip, on the other hand, had been born in a private maternity hospital back in Brisbane, because Frances had been terrified of having her child on an isolated Outback station. Uncle Aaron, who he sort of remembered as kind, had been killed on the station, handling a wild steer, when Philip was just a little boy. The steer had gored him. Aaron had died without uttering a cry.

After that they had all lived in hell.

*   *   *

"Well, don't you look pretty!" Brock stood in the open doorway staring down at Shelley, the delicate fastidiousness of her. She had braided her beautiful red hair so it coiled and glinted around her small head like loops of flame, complementing flawless skin smooth as a baby's. A slick of bright colour decorated her mouth, and her green eyes were so big and mysterious they dominated her face. She looked as if he could cast spells if she so chose at any moment—even on him.

Watch out!

The thought made him laugh aloud. "'Light she was and like a fairy!' Brock spoke with an exaggerated Irish accent. "That's an extremely pretty blouse." Extremely pretty breasts. He felt a sudden wave of desire that made his stomach tighten into a hard knot. But he was obsessively involved with regaining his birthright, remember? Hadn't he already decided he couldn't get involved with Shelley Logan? Yet in the space of half an hour he had developed quite a taste for her.

Brock's gaze moving over her left Shelley with a sensation of shivery excitement. He had one arm lazily resting above her head on the doorjamb, and was just staring down at her. He was so tall.

"I'm glad you like it." It cost an effort but her voice came out normally. "I didn't have anything suitable to wear so I raced down to the local dress shop. I found this in the nick of time."

"My good fortune." He grinned. "Shall we go? I've made reservations. They tell me Harriet's menus are so great people have to book ahead."

"Did you speak to Harriet herself?" She had to break through this confusion, this spell, otherwise the excitement would be impossible to stop.

He took the key of the door from her fingers. "That's how we've managed to get in. Harriet told me she'd look after us. Harriet's a big fan of yours."

"That works both ways." She looked at the span of his

shoulders as he closed her door, suddenly bedevilled by the memory of what it was like to be swept up in his arms. Yet something about Brock Tyson, for all his macho image, made her heart break. What a dreadful penance it must have been for his mother and him, having to remain on Mulgaree after his father had deserted them. It was such a sad house. Like her own.

"I've not been to Harriet's since it opened," she remarked, pitching her tone to conversational. "I was invited to the gala night, but Amanda wanted to go and I wasn't happy leaving my mother. You wouldn't believe the migraines she gets."

He took her arm as they walked the corridor, so slender, so delicate, he felt he could encircle it. "How we sacrifice our lives to misery."

"My mother is afraid to be happy. She believes that it would be a disloyalty to Sean."

"Sounds a terrible waste. It's depressing, but I can't say I don't understand," he replied sombrely.

They had to move past a sea of smiling, highly interested faces on their way out of the pub. Everyone seemed thrilled to have Brock back. Brock was quite calm with it all, returning shouted greetings from the bar. Shelley felt herself blush. What was she doing on Brock Tyson's arm? Just being with him seemed a tremendous event.

They walked in a vaguely fraught silence until they reached Harriet's, where lights from the restaurant spilled out onto the pavement. Inside it was lovely and cool, the décor green and white, with feathery stands of bamboo in pots, graceful arches, and old sepia photographs of the town's past decorating a wall. From the night it had opened Harriet's had been a very popular gathering place for the locals as well as people from the outlying stations.

Harriet, looking marvellous in a mandarin-yellow Thai silk caftan that flowed softly around her slim body, came forward to greet them jauntily.

"Welcome, welcome!" She bent forward to kiss her ex-pupil Shelley's cheek. "Where have you been all this time, Brock? We've really missed you."

"Ireland." He looked into Harriet's eyes, finding them kind and very shrewd. He named a famous stud farm.

She nodded, having heard of it. "The life must have agreed with you. You look marvellous. But someone told me as I came up that you lost your dear mother?"

For a minute he couldn't answer, grief and wildness spoiling in him. "She's where she wanted to be, Harriet. The home of her ancestors. There was no home for her here." Pain and bitterness played about his chiselled mouth.

"My heart aches for you, Brock. You've taken a hard blow." Harriet pressed his arm, looking with great sympathy into his brilliant eyes. "We'll talk of this again, but for now you'll be wanting to find some peace and comfort. I have a good table for you in the courtyard. Come through. You look lovely, Shelley."

Harriet smiled with great encouragement at her. Shelley was a young woman she very much admired. A brave person of high intelligence, Shelley Logan could have gone far in any one of the big cities, but she had stuck with her highly dysfunctional, unappreciative family. What it was to be tied by the bonds of love and loyalty! And a quite undeserved feeling of guilt, Harriet thought.

"Great to see you, Brock!"

Brock's hand was caught and held over and over, slowing their progress, but finally they were seated at a secluded table for two in the courtyard, with its white rattan glass-topped tables and white rattan chairs and huge golden canes in glazed pots. The comfortable upholstery was in white Indian cotton with a pattern of green bamboo leaves to continue the theme, while near them white ceramic elephants held pots of colourful flowers on their backs. It all looked enormously attractive.

The restaurant was only open three times a week—after all Harriet was well into her sixties and couldn't risk burnout—on Wednesday, Friday and Saturday, for lunch and dinner. But far from stretching her to the limit, Shelley thought affectionately, Harriet looked years younger and on top of the world.

"An experience awaits you," Harriet was saying with a flourish, passing them what looked like a fairly extensive menu for a small restaurant. "Oriental-style cooking is the speciality of the house, but if you would like something else we can whip it up for you."

"You're a wonder, Miss Crompton," Brock told her, his face respectful but still holding more than a trace of that wicked daring that had so distinguished him as a boy.

"Tell me that when your meal is over." Harriet smiled. "Now, I must return to the kitchen—but one of my girls will be here shortly to take your order. Would you care for a drink in the meantime?"

"Shelley?" Brock looked across the table at his companion, so pretty he had no desire to look anywhere else.

"May I have a glass of white wine?"

"Certainly. Why don't we push the boat out and have champagne?" It had been a rotten day. He could do with a few bubbles, and Shelley might like it. "Okay?"

"Perfect," Shelley agreed.

Harriet smiled. "I'll have someone bring it over."

CHAPTER TWO

OVER the leisurely meal Brock left the soul-destroying
world of Mulgaree with all its bleak memories behind him.
Shelley was lovely enough for any man—so interested in
what he was saying, asking such intelligent questions that
he found his whole body, for months coiled tight as a spring,
relaxing. And dinner rated highly. He'd had some fine, unforgettable meals in the gourmet restaurants of Ireland and
France, where he'd visited constantly on the stud farm's
business, but the well-travelled Harriet was right up there
with them. No mean feat for a small Outback town on the
edge of nowhere.

They'd opted for Thai food, as it was the speciality of
the house: magnificent chilli prawns, flown in from the tropical north, garnished with crispy curry leaves and served
with a wonderfully flavoured cream sauce, followed by a
chicken dish in a peanut sauce, accompanied by shredded
cucumber, carrots and spring onions. Then they'd enjoyed
little jellied fruits, beautifully arranged, to finish. Delicious,
imaginative and innovative, when most dishes were done to
death.

"That was superb!" Brock said with satisfaction and not
a little surprise.

"I've never had such a wonderful meal in my life!"
Shelley agreed. "I've been flat out trying to master a few
Japanese dishes for my guests."

"Have you succeeded?" He was deriving a lot of pleasure from watching the swift changes of expression on her
mobile face. In the candleglow from the frangipani-ringed
lamp her eyes had little flecks of gold suspended in the
emerald. Fascinating!

"It's taken time," she said. "I've certainly mastered su-shi rice, but the rice only lasts a day. You can only serve it once. The biggest problem is getting in fresh fish—frozen simply won't do. Most times I have to make do with canned salmon and crab, but our plentiful beef is the basis for su-kiyaki, teriyaki, kushi-age. I've even bought special serving ware—bowls, plates, platters. They're white. Food always looks good on white. Not to mention accessories like om-elette pans. Japanese omelettes need a special rectangular pan. I'm good with thin and thick omelettes, and I'm not bad with presentation."

He smiled at her enthusiasm. "I'll have to visit some time," he said, making a decision to do just that. "I seem to recall you had an artistic streak at school. Didn't Miss Crompton keep all your drawings?"

"She did." Shelley felt a tingle of pleasure. "Fancy your remembering that. I still have my drawing and my water-colours, whenever I get the time for relaxation. I'm a thwarted botanical artist. You'd be surprised at the remote areas I've ventured into when all the wildflowers are out."

"You sound like you really love what you do." She looked so happy he wanted to reach over and take her hand. Seemingly so fragile, she sizzled with life.

"Of course. I'm not as certain as Miss Crompton my watercolours are that good, but she seems to think so. She taught me art and its appreciation in the first place. Encouraged me every step of the way. Told me I was way better than she was years ago! She's been trying to get me to mount an exhibition. She even offered to have it here." Shelley glanced about the courtyard and into the packed main room. "Imagine my watercolours all over her walls, like a gallery."

"That sounds like an excellent idea." Brock realized with surprise he was getting a considerable lift out of Shelley's company, when beautiful, experienced women with lan-guorous eyes had come close to boring him. "I'm quite sure Miss Crompton is an excellent judge."

Shelley smiled. "That's what gives me confidence. Harriet has done me such a lot of good. I love painting on silk as well. One of these days I'm going to find my way up to the Daintree. I want to paint the rainforest flora and the butterflies. The brilliant electric blue Ulysses and all the lacewings. Butterflies are so romantic! But, there; you're making me talk too much."

"Believe me, I'm enjoying it. Keep going." The tension had all but drained out of him. He might even see if he couldn't organise a trip to the Daintree for her some time.

"Stop me at any time," she advised. "I'll never run out of things to paint. There's a whole world of tropical birds, and all the fruits of the rainforest."

"How are you going to fit all this in?" he mocked.

"Heaven knows! Most times I'm run off my feet."

"There's certainly nothing of you." He controlled his tone, but he could tell just by looking at her she'd be exquisite to make love to. He had a finely honed instinct about such things.

"Don't be fooled," she replied. "I'm strong and I eat properly—as you can see. It's a lot of work, but I really enjoy the tourist parties. I get a huge amount of pleasure out of my work, too. It was a Japanese lady who spent a lot of time showing me how to wield a vegetable knife to make all the beautiful garnishes that adorn Japanese food platters. Now, she *was* an artist. She could make anything of simple vegetables, flowers, leaves, little ornaments—you name it. Just give her a lemon or a lime, a cucumber, a radish, mushroom, zucchini, baby squash. It was marvellous just to watch her."

"I expect it took her years to master the technique."

She nodded. "Getting to know the Japanese and their language has been a real experience. Learning to prepare Japanese food is one good way of entering the culture."

"So you're open to all outside influences? Though Australia nowadays is very much part of Asia. You really are the hostess with the mostest!"

"I try to be. We desperately need our paying guests. I've been trying to talk one of our aboriginal stockmen, a tribal elder, into taking the guests for bush walks to the Wybourne caves. They're so careful and appreciative of the fragile environment. So far Dad has kept him busy, but it would take a lot off me."

"It sounds like you relish a challenge, Shelley?" Brock tilted his wine glass, watching the fine beads rising.

"Especially when the challenge pays off. I suppose it's far too early for you to formulate any plans—unless you intend to return to Ireland?" She prepared herself to be tremendously disappointed if he said yes.

"My plan is to take over the Kingsley chain."

At his tone she inhaled deeply. There was such bitterness in his brilliant eyes. "Forgive me, Brock, but is that possible?" she dared ask. "There's Philip after all."

"I don't take partners," he said, with a very sardonic expression.

Something about him scared her. "Then I'll pray for you."

"Do that." Suddenly he smiled, an illuminating flash like a ray of sunshine through storm clouds. "I may need it. Please don't look at me with fear in your eyes, Shelley Logan."

"I'm fearful for you," she said. "How could your grandfather possibly change?"

He gripped the stem of the wine glass so tightly she though it might shatter. "Maybe he's discovered he's got a conscience after all."

"You believe he means to reinstate you in his will?" She was very aware of the shift in his mood.

He nodded, though his mouth had a sceptical twist. "I'm always troubled by my grandfather's motives, Shelley. On the face of it he's told me he wants a reconciliation, but he's always been the most devious of men. Maybe it's another cruel joke. Maybe he's a little mad these days. Pain is tearing his body to pieces. Guilt his mind. He was even talking of going to Ireland to visit my mother's grave. He'll never get there.''

"He's that bad?'' Shelley waited quietly for his reply.

"Even if he survived the journey he knows what kind of a reception he'd get from my mother's people and all the friends we made. He put my mother through dreadful anguish. Though she eventually found peace I'm sure all those terrible years took their toll.''

"He must have loved her once.''

His answer was suave and cutting. "My grandfather knows nothing about love, Shelley.''

"I'm so terribly sorry, Brock. Maybe you shouldn't have come back when there's so much turbulence inside you.''

"There was no alternative,'' he answered, as though her comment had touched a raw nerve. "Can you see it? The turbulence?''

"I'm sad to say yes!'' She spoke truthfully, even if it wasn't something he cared to hear. "I've been watching you all night.'' It was there in the tautness of his features, the way his hands tended to clench whenever his grandfather's name was mentioned.

"Then no doubt you're right!'' His voice was suave. "There's no help for my bitterness, I'm afraid, but Mulgaree is part of me. It's my turn to close in. And no way am I going to allow Philip and Frances to cut me out.''

"Am I saying the wrong thing every time I open my mouth?'' she asked wryly. "I do understand your feelings, Brock, but you must have considered Philip has a legitimate claim? He's Rex Kingsley's grandson too. You really couldn't tolerate sharing Mulgaree?''

He reached out suddenly and grasped her hand. It sent shock waves racing down her arm. "Philip, my dear Shelley, isn't competent to run Mulgaree, let alone the whole chain. Consider that. I've only been back a couple of days and it's perfectly plain Philip can't manage. He doesn't know how to use his power, position or money. He's no good with the men. You can't demand respect; you have to

earn it. It wouldn't take him long to lose what Kingsley has
built up. Using part of the Brockway fortune, I'll remind
you." His jaw looked tight enough to crack.

"Brock, you're hurting me."

"I'm sorry." He released her hand immediately, still with
the glint in his eyes.

"How bad is your grandfather?" She well remembered a
big, handsome, scowling, arrogant man.

He glanced away. "He tells me his heart has got a hell
of a big leak in it, his brain's on the edge and cancer is
eating away at his stomach. His death could be any time,
damn him."

She gave an involuntary little shudder. "That sounds so
harsh and unforgiving."

His eyes burned over her. "If it is, it's the result of his
treatment of me and my mother. Sorry, Shelley." He
shrugged. "I'm too far gone for a sweet little thing like you
to reform me."

"I'm not all that sweet," she said briskly. "Not for a
long time. Like you, I'm capable of holding deep resent-
ments. I'm only saying don't let your grief and your bitterness gobble you up. Then your grandfather will win. You
could even end up like him."

"What a thought!" he said tautly. "And yet you can say
it to my face!"

"The truth isn't always what we want to hear. I'm sorry
if I upset you, Brock. It wasn't my intention."

His handsome mouth twisted. "It wasn't? For a little bit
of a thing you pack quite a punch. But then I expect you
know as much about bitterness as I do. Didn't your family
condemn you?"

It was her turn to suffer. "You have a cruel streak." She
gazed at him with expressive green eyes.

"So be warned."

"And don't you intrude upon my inner world either,"
Shelley continued, doing her best to ignore the sexual tension that simmered between them.

He answered in an ironic voice. "Shelley, both our lives might just as well have been splashed across the front pages of the town gazette. Everyone knows our history."

"How could they not?" she countered, with a touch of his own bitterness. "Sometimes I think I'll never be free. Losing my twin in such tragic circumstances has coloured my life grey."

"Then you have to change it." He spoke emphatically. "No one with flame-coloured hair should ever lead a dull life. You can't let your family cage you. You're entitled to a life of your own. But hopefully not with my cousin. That would be too, too awful."

Brock looked up, and as he did so vertical lines appeared between his black brows.

"Speak of the devil!" he groaned. "You're not going to believe this, but Philip is on his way over to our table."

"No!" Mechanically she turned her head. "Oh, my goodness!"

"Exactly," Brock muttered, a hard timbre to his voice.

Philip Kingsley made it to their table. He was a tall, sober young man, his shoulders slightly stooped, as if under a weight. He had the well-cut Kingsley features that would have been striking had they had some edge to them. As it was he was merely good-looking. Beside his cousin Brock, with his dark, handsome smoulder, Philip looked decidedly soft.

He looked down at her with an expression like betrayal in his hazel eyes. "Evening, Shelley! You're the very last person I expected to see here with Brock!" He employed an accusatory tone that irritated Shelley immensely, then, without being asked, pulled a spare chair to the table and sat down. "Why in the world would you be having dinner with *Brock*?" he asked, looking at her in dismay.

She reacted with a lick of temper. "Philip, do me a favour. It's none of your business." The air was so electric it crackled with static.

"I thought you'd given me to understand it was?" he retorted, moving his chair even closer.

"I certainly have not." She spoke quietly, but through clenched teeth.

"I'm sorry. I thought you had," he persisted, which she knew was his way. Persistence would win the day.

Brock held up a silencing hand "For heaven's sake, Phil, stop hassling the girl. You heard what Shelley said. What would she want with a pompous stuffed shirt like you? Come to that, what in hell are you doing here? I don't recall inviting you to sit at our table." There was a distinctly aggressive edge to Brock's voice, a warning darkening his expression.

"Is something wrong at home, Philip?" Shelley swiftly cut in. "Is that it?" Clearly there was no love lost between the cousins.

Philip looked directly at her, his soul in his eyes. "Grandfather has had a bad turn. He's asking for Brock. I would have explained if you'd given me time."

Shelley's sparkling gaze softened. "You should have spoken right off, instead of taking me to task. So that's the purpose of your trip?"

"If it's true." Brock shrugged. "It's probably Kingsley's way to get me back to the house. He wants us all closed up together. Preferably at each other's throats."

Philip shook his narrow head. "Can't you try to be a little bit more compassionate towards Grandfather?" he said, his face flushed.

"No, sorry. He used up all the compassion I had long ago."

"The great wonder is that he wants you home at all," Philip said with a censure Shelley found quite bizarre and certainly dishonest. Every time she and Philip had been together Philip had been very vocal regarding his own load of resentment against his grandfather. He had always seemed desperate to win her sympathy—which, up until now, he'd received in good measure.

Brock treated his cousin to a cynical smile. "Phil, you old hypocrite!" he scoffed.

"We're talking about our grandfather." Philip lifted a sanctimonious hand. "He was a Colossus. Now he lies in bed, just staring at the ceiling. I hate to see him cut down like that. He's been so strong. Invincible. It's awful to see him so terribly reduced." His voice was low and husky. "It's killing me."

Brock's mouth twitched. "Hell, it's a wonder you're not gushing tears."

"You're such a heartless bastard!"

"And you're such a phony you make me want to puke."

"You have no sense of family," Philip flashed back, as though Brock had left a black stain on the Kingsley good name. "It's no wonder Grandfather sent you and Aunt Catherine packing."

The colour seemed to drain from Brock's dark polished skin, and for a ghastly instant Shelley wondered whether he would leap for his cousin's throat.

"Take no notice, Brock." She made a grab for his hand, holding it as tightly as she could. "Why don't you leave, Philip? You've delivered your message."

Philip's whole body stiffened. "I can't believe you're taking Brock's part against me. You're my friend. Not his."

"You make that sound like Shelley's your property," Brock drawled, somehow moving back from furious anger. Who would have thought a small, feminine hand could hold him in such a hard crunch? Shelley Logan had to be taken seriously, he thought, abruptly amused.

"We have plans for the future," Philip announced. "I'm very different to you, Brock. I want to make something of my life."

A look of disdain came into Brock's eyes. "Then you'll have your work cut out, because you're a gutless wonder. You hate that man just as much as I do. He's made your life hell, but here you are trying to portray yourself as his noble, grieving grandson. No bets on what you and your

mother are after. Kingsley Holdings. That's why you set out
to discredit and undermine me. God knows how you can
shake off the guilt and the shame.''

''I've no idea what you're talking about,'' Philip said
sharply, but he was unable to meet his cousin's challenging
stare.

''The plotting, Phil. The stories you carried to Kingsley.
What did it matter that you couldn't prove them? God, you
two must have held a big party when we left.''

''Got kicked out, don't you mean?'' Philip sneered.
''Grandfather gave you every chance. No one plotted
against you. It was you who deliberately set out to anger
and upset him. The sooner you realize that, the better. You
didn't know how to conduct yourself as a Kingsley should.
You were wild. Wild from childhood.''

''Then you and your mother had nothing to worry about,
did you? Except she had the brains to cotton on that you
couldn't measure up. Wild old me was cramping your style.
I had to go. In retrospect, I'd call it an escape. It seems to
me you're the one who's led the soul-destroying life. And
thoroughly deserved it, don't you think?''

''Grandfather wants you home,'' Philip replied doggedly,
his face stiff and expressionless.

''Surely you're not here to collect me?'' There was a
shade of amusement in Brock's eyes.

''I have the helicopter.'' Philip glanced at Shelley, and
then swiftly glanced away, as if the sight of her gave him
pain.

''I've no intention of going back with you.'' Brock was
direct. ''I'll come back to Mulgaree when I'm ready. That'll
be tomorrow.''

''What if tomorrow's too late?'' Philip was roused to ask,
leaning forward with his elbows on the table.

''C'est la vie!'' Brock gave a truly Gallic shrug, his accent confirming he'd devoted time and attention to learning
the French language. ''But I don't imagine that it will be.

Kingsley will chose his exact moment to die. Only a handful of people can do that," he added, with grudging admiration.

"You realize what it cost me to make this trip?" Philip complained. "To track you down here?" He threw another despairing glance in Shelley's direction, as though she were guilty of serious disloyalty.

"Why the desperation?" Brock's luminescent eyes narrowed. "Wouldn't it be in your interests to report that I've said I'll come when I'm good and ready?"

"Don't think I won't. You've got a strange way of trying to engineer a reconciliation," Philip said.

"And you're still doing your mother's dirty work." Brock was clearly running out of patience.

Not even thick-skinned Philip could stay any longer. He raised himself up from the table, shaking his head dismally. He turned to Shelley imploringly.

"Looks like you're finished. Could I walk you back to the hotel, Shelley? There's something I need to talk to you about privately."

Brock leaned back in his chair. "Is he serious?" he asked, directing a sparkling glance at Shelley. "Goodbye, Phil."

Philip leaned down, speaking very quietly. "And you can go to hell."

"I'm not going to hell, Phil." Brock lifted clear, daunting eyes. "I'm putting my house in order. But give me one good reason why you shouldn't."

"I'm just as big a victim as ever you were," Philip said, very bitterly for someone who'd just avowed love and concern for his grandfather.

"I know that, Phil." Brock waved his hand in dismissal.

"Don't think I'll let you win. I haven't slaved all these years for nothing. I won't take it."

"Me neither."

Philip continued to stand, obviously struggling for control. Shelley felt a thrust of pity. "Just go, Philip. Don't say any more. People are looking this way."

"Let them," Philip said, body rigid, face bitter. "I

thought I was certain of you, Shelley. Certain of the sort of person you were. Now I'm less certain."

"That could be a plus," she said crisply. "Please go."

"I will." His tone suggested she had fallen far in his estimation. "Don't be fool enough to trust my cousin. Brock and his reputation with the girls go back a long way."

"I always made sure I didn't hurt anyone," Brock remarked, having the last word.

Harriet was seated on a white lattice-backed chair behind the cash register, attending to the bills of her departing guests. When his turn came Brock pulled out a handful of dollars and handed it to her. "That was an outstanding meal, Miss Crompton. We thoroughly enjoyed it."

Harriet smiled back, but her grey eyes were searching. "Everything all right? I'm sorry, but I had to tell Philip where you were."

Brock shrugged. "Don't worry about it."

"He told me your grandfather's condition is worsening," Harriet said quietly into the lull, including Shelley in her glance.

"I guess I'll find out when I get back."

"I hope things go well for you, Daniel."

Brock laughed. "Gosh, doesn't that take me back! I think you're the only person in Koomera Crossing who ever called me Daniel."

"You look like a Daniel," Harriet said. "Daniel in the lions' den. I've got to warn you. Nothing's changed."

"You mean with the old man?"

"And the rest of the family."

"Tell me something I don't know, Miss Crompton."

"That's not much, I imagine," Harriet said wryly, thinking the striking young man in front of her had had a very rough childhood and adolescence. Far worse than his cousin, Philip, who never did a solitary thing to try his grandfather's very limited patience.

"How are things on Wybourne, Shelley?" Harriet asked

as they settled up. "I hear you can't keep up with business?"

"We've another party of Japanese tourists due in a month," Shelley confirmed.

"Aren't you an enterprising young woman? But I never thought you'd get into this business. If you're ever pushed and you need help let me know. I mean that, Shelley."

"I know you do, Miss Crompton. Thank you." Shelley reached over the high counter and touched Harriet's fragile wrist. "You're a good friend." She moved back as other diners approached the lobby.

"Don't forget about our showing." Harriet reminded Shelley of their discussion.

"When I've got time."

"It'll be fun! Come again!" Harriet called.

On their way back to the hotel they stopped to sit on a park bench. The sky was swept with stars, a huge silver moon bathing the little oasis in a dreamlike radiance. A white haze hung over the creek, the broad sheet of water filled with spangled reflections.

Shelley ran her hands down her arms. A cool wind from the desert, where it was always cold at night, rushed through the darkly coloured trees, sending long shadows and spent leaves dancing across the broad expanse of grass. They weren't far off the street, with its old-fashioned lamps in full bloom, yet Shelley felt very much alone with Brock. It was as if no one and nothing existed but them. Even the noise of the town, tonight full of people, had faded away.

As Brock remained silent, obviously lost in thought, Shelley tilted her head towards the dazzling sky. The stars were like tiny blazing fires in that black velvet backdrop. She had no difficulty at all picking out her favourite constellations. The galaxy of the Milky Way, a broad diamond-encrusted avenue, Orion the mighty hunter, Pleiades, the Seven Sisters in the constellation Taurus, the Southern Cross, worshipped by the aboriginal people. These constel-

lations had looked down on the Great South Land since the
dawn of creation.

"What do the skies over Ireland look like?" she asked
softly, unable to shake the feeling of a most wonderful isolation. Just the two of them.

It took a moment for Brock to reply. In truth, though he'd
loved his time in Ireland, with its close family ties, his heart
had hungered for his desert home. "Not like ours. They
don't have this immense clarity. Nothing can match our desert sky. By day a blazing cloudless blue, by night an overwhelming glory. A man can almost reach up and grasp a
pocketful of fabulous jewels.

"Ireland is another world, Shelley. It's teeming with a
different kind of beauty. Australia would seem a stupendous
size to an Irishman, as it would have to the early settlers.
Our landscape, with an immense wilderness at its heart, is
savage compared with theirs. Ours is vast in size, where
theirs is small and contained.

"That country and its people inspire both love and sorrow. My grandmother's relatives took us under their wing.
They couldn't have been warmer or more supportive, or
more brilliantly funny. They're great storytellers and they're
wonderfully skilled with horses. But as to the climate!
Outback people like us would think we were on another
planet. Unlike here, where a single downpour is a divine
blessing, it actually rains all the time there. Not great tor-
rential floods, like here, but a perennial fine mist.
Consequently the countryside is always emerald-green.
You'd be right at home there, Shelley. Like Leanan-Sidhe,
the muse of poets."

"Is she a water faerie?" she asked, with a sense of being
caught up in something outside her control.

"No, but she's a very lovely creature indeed, with long
floating red hair and emerald eyes."

"As long as she's not a water sprite," Shelley said,
stabbed by a grief never far from her. "Their sole delight
is drowning children."

Instinctively Brock found himself encircling her shoulders. "How did I get onto that theme? Insensitive fool that I am."

"No, it's all right." She shook her head. "Our grandmother, Moira, was forever filling our heads with fairy tales. Some of them were scary, but she used to tell them all the same. One of her stories was about the Asrai. They're delicate little female faeries who swim up to the surface of lakes and waterholes and billabongs to capture your attention. But as soon as you put out your hand they melt away. I've often thought maybe Sean saw one. Some beautiful little creature, almost visible. He just had to lean in. Something pulled him down to a watery grave."

"Don't break my heart, Shelley," Brock warned, drawing her closer to his body. This was no streamlined seduction, but an inherent tenderness he was mostly at pains to hide. "What heart I have left." His tone dipped ironically.

"We're damaged people, Brock," she murmured as the thought came to her.

"Childhood trauma has abiding effects," he agreed, total empathy in his voice. "But you should have been helped to find your way out of it." Somehow her red-gold head had sunk onto his shoulder—or had he placed it there? Most probably, but she wasn't pulling away. "My story's not like yours, Shelley, though we both come from badly integrated families. Have you never spoken to anyone—a professional—about your childhood trauma and the time since?"

"Who could I speak to, Brock? I lead an isolated existence. I never even have need to see a doctor, though I admire and respect Dr Sarah at Koomera Bush Hospital. She tries hard to help my mother, but Mum has joined forces with her terrible depression. She won't make the attempt to fight out of it. And Dad is very bitter about life. He lost his son. His only son. Sons are important to a man, especially a man like Dad. If it had come to choosing which twin had to be sacrificed it would have been me, no question."

"How do you continue to love him when he leaves you

out in the emotional cold?'' he asked with a rush of impatience.

She stiffened slightly.

"Don't go away.'' His hand soothed her.

"My parents continue to suffer, Brock,'' she pointed out, her body relaxing. "They don't need me to hate them.''

"Which makes you a little saint?'' His tone was dry.

"I didn't say I don't have my bad days when I'm faced with the question: What am I doing staying around, working so hard?'' she retorted. "It's such a struggle, yet no one seems to care. Far from being a saint—and I know you're having a go at me—I have an underlying anger at the way I'm treated. But I guess the bottom line is I'll never abandon my family.''

"Surely you'll marry?'' he asked crisply. "One wonders why some enterprising guy—which automatically excludes my cousin—hasn't swept you off your feet already?''

"Perhaps he'd recognise I come with too much baggage to allow for any real development,'' she suggested, straightening before she found herself lying against his chest.

"I saw Philip's face tonight. I'd say he was very much in love with you. Just seeing you with me blew him apart.''

She was desperately aware of his closeness, his arm lying along the park bench just behind her shoulders, the glimmer of his pale shirt, the male scent of him. "I can't help the fact Philip has formed an attachment. Ours is a relatively small community and he's partnered me at dances. We see one another at every social occasion. We talk a lot. But, I repeat, there's no love affair that I'm aware of.''

"You'd better tell him that,'' he said bluntly.

"Anyway, his mother thinks he should drop me. I'm not good enough.'' She said it with a trace of black humour.

"Then she's got very poor judgement. Say, you're shivering. Are you cold?''

She rubbed her bare arms. They were faintly chilled by the desert breeze. "When we start walking I'll warm up. This blouse is quite sheer.''

"Just the sort of blouse I like." His voice was a deep purr. "Listen, I'm sorry I don't have anything to put around your shoulders. Except my arm, of course. So come along, Shelley." He stood up, extended his hand. "We'll make our way back to the pub."

The friendly gallantry should have worked. They should have gone on their way with nothing sexual to complicate the evening. Only that never happened. Brock was a man on the edge, his hard desire for this spirited little redhead spiralling.

Even the wind was his co-conspirator. Gradually it had increased in strength, becoming a whirling force. It began to tug at her hair. Though she immediately put up her hand it had no difficulty loosening the pins that held the glittery loops in place. It slid and uncoiled through her fingers.

He hadn't reckoned on this, so he wasn't really to blame, was he? Her ability to move him, to capture his attention when he knew he should disengage, quite simply overrode his best intentions. He didn't need or want involvement, but the sight of her with her arms behind her head, tussling with her beautiful long windblown hair, her slender body in a spin in an effort to throw off curling skeins that lashed her face with silk, played on his erotic imagination, giving him immense pleasure.

Her laughter was so young, so carefree, like ripples of silver. Surely it summoned any red-blooded man to pull her into his arms?

A tremble ran down his strong forearms. He imagined her in his embrace even before she was there. There was no question of pausing, of caution, or even catching his breath. He gave his passionate nature full rein, taking small comfort in the fact that he hadn't planned any of it. This was a means to assuage his sick hunger, the griefs that could destroy him.

Heart torn, he hauled her to him so it was impossible for her to escape, stopping her laughing mouth with his own, feeling the impact run through his body like flame. For an instant her soft lips didn't move beneath his—he'd shocked

her—but he parted them with his tongue, whispering her
name into her open mouth.

"Shelley!" It was a marvellous feeling. The child he had
known the whole of her life had turned into a beguiling
woman. A woman with enough power to bewitch him.

"What are you doing, Brock?" Shelley gasped, overcome
by sensation. Even the moon and stars faded to nothing.
There was only his body, his hands, his mouth. His physical
presence so familiar to her, yet totally foreign.

"Kissing you," he muttered, struggling with the torment
to go further. He should stop, but he couldn't. Not from the
moment he found her lips.

Only she was so unprepared for it. "Wait." She put a
hand to his chest.

"Wait what? Am I going too fast for you?"

She ought to say, yes, but the mounting forces seemed
colossal.

He pulled her back to him, drinking her in like a draught
of wine.

She sounded a tiny bit frightened. A man could never
assume anything and he was carrying her along too fast. But
the male drive to know the female was vibrating through
him, subduing her to the extent she seemed at a loss to stop
him.

He held her face up to his, his tongue plunging deeper,
drinking her in like a draught of wine. Heat sizzled along
his veins like a fever, but it was a fever he was eager to
suffer.

She was so beautiful. So sensitive. So right. He wanted
to lift her. Carry her away. Show her what lovemaking was
all about.

His hand moved to the porcelain skin of her throat, where
a pulse beat so full and fast it betrayed her. Her delicate
neck was flushed with agitation and excitement. His hands
were frantic to move lower, to take full possession of her
breasts, to find the rosebud nipples swollen in arousal. He
forced them to stay where they were, when they wanted to

range over her body, stroke naked skin. In a moment he would go too dangerously far when all he'd meant to do was walk her back to the hotel and the safety of her own bed.

This was Shelley Logan he was plying with fierce, insistent kisses and caresses. Had he forgotten? Her body was rippling now, at his every stroke. She was panting a little, leaning into him, her beautiful hair all over her face, his face. He could inhale its clean scent. He knew he had only to apply a little more pressure, but a kind of purity attended her.

He released her so abruptly Shelley was obliged to make a grab for his shirt.

"Brock!" She held tight to him, disoriented, genuinely worried for a moment that she might faint. She didn't feel solid at all, but floating. Every part of her he had touched was scintillating, aglow.

"I didn't mean that to happen." His own speech was rough with emotion.

"I never dreamed you did." This was far beyond anything she had experienced before.

"But you wanted me to."

"Did I?" She pressed a hand to her breast. Her heart was beating crazily. "I thought you were going to kiss me until morning."

"Believe me, I want to," he said edgily. "But I had to decide against it."

She tried hard to adjust to his abrupt change of mood. "Would it be too much to ask why?"

"You want the truth?" He stared down at her with intensity. "You're simply too sweet, too soft, too succulent. And I'm too hungry. I couldn't have it ending in tears."

In brief seconds Shelley found the strength to stand clear of his lean, powerful body. "You won't be getting any tears from me, Brock," she said, putting a lot of fire into it. "Your innumerable conquests have gone to your head. It's not the first time you've kissed me, anyway, and I've managed to survive.''

"Well, was that better or worse than the last time?" He took a step towards her, but she took a corresponding step back.

"Let's say it was marginally better than shaking hands.''

"That's why you couldn't stand by yourself for a few moments?'' he taunted. "I don't want to upset you, but now's not the time to run off the rails—even if I'd like nothing more. My future is under threat.''

"Not from me,'' she rejoined.

He gave a wince. "That was as sharp as a slap.''

"You deserved it!'' Finally she managed to subdue her hair. "Let's forget about it, shall we? I know I can.''

His laugh was mocking. "Don't get mortally offended, but I don't think you'll find it as easy as all that.''

"Won't I?'' She put out a flat hand and pushed him in the chest. "I'm a very disciplined person, Brock Tyson, you devil.''

"Really? A devil?'' He locked his fingers around her wrist. "Think about it. I could have taken that further.''

"I bet you do that a lot!''

"Well, tonight I just couldn't handle it.'' He spoke with so much self-mockery she blushed. "Have you any idea how beautiful you are?''

This was a man who could melt a woman without laying a hand on her. "You're the one having difficulties, not me,'' she countered. "Are you going to let go of me?''

"No.'' He raised her hand lingeringly to his mouth. "But I am going to walk you back safely to the pub. Isn't that the decent thing?''

"Next you're going to tell me I'm different to every other girl you've ever met,'' she said tartly.

"Well, of course you are.'' He sounded amused. "You're the only girl I've ever kissed who doesn't keep her eyes closed.''

CHAPTER THREE

SHELLEY drove right up to the front steps of the homestead, trying to forget just how long and hot the trip had been. Her big concern on the journey had been dust storms. They were inevitable in a time of drought, when the wind picked up the Interior's precious top soil and dumped millions of tonnes of it a thousand miles away in the ocean. She'd lived through quite a few dust storms, some of considerable severity. They desperately needed rain, but though the whole Outback prayed, they weren't getting any. The skies above her were a hard enamelled cobalt with not a single cloud on the horizon.

If it hadn't been for the permanent waterholes and billabongs on the station she'd have had to toss the whole idea of running Outback Adventures out of the window. The bores served their purpose, but in the Dry they sent fountains of near boiling water high into the air.

She wished there was someone there to help unload. There was no use hoping Amanda would help her. Amanda—and she was seriously disgusted with her sister about this—was bone-lazy. In the heat she acted like wax to a flame. It was a real con too, the way Amanda always complained of her bad back and her fears of hurting it.

Amanda found any way there was of avoiding physical toil, though she spent extravagant amounts of time lying around waiting for life to happen. She didn't in fact get out of bed before ten. She wrote songs. Some were good. She played the piano and guitar, both well. Shelley herself had never qualified for music lessons.

"Why do you ask when you know money's tight?" her father had always said, turning away as though he couldn't bear to look at her too long. As if all she evoked was memories of her twin.

Well, at least she'd had one heck of an experience last night. A blazing bonfire of the senses. Brock Tyson was dangerous, his sexual prowess legendary. If she hadn't been certain of it before, she was now.

And what of Philip? Philip had gone out of his way to suggest there was a romance between them. She would have said he had seemed driven to do it, probably for Brock's benefit, just to let his cousin know she was taken. Not that Brock had taken the slightest heed of the warning, if that was what it had been. It might even have been an act of sheer devilment.

The fact remained that everything was different now—a violent shift in their relationship. Not that she'd ever been one of Brock Tyson's girls. She'd still been a student, years younger than him. And now he had to go and pique her by telling her he wasn't looking for involvement. The cheek of him!

Yet she'd spent the whole night tossing and turning, reliving the unprecedented excitement of his performance and her humiliating response. That was black magic... She had imagined he had come to her, bent over her, his arms curving beneath her body. He was the lover she wanted.

She was out of her mind!

Her head, her heart, her blood and nerves were still tingling from the rain of kisses, though a full ten hours had gone by and she was back in her world, with its massive ongoing problems.

They'd said little to each other on the short journey back to the hotel, walking in a fraught silence, but she'd wished the moonlit road would stretch forever. Brock had told her he'd be leaving very early in the morning but that he would take up her offer to visit Wybourne some time. That was if she could clear it with her father. He'd laughed a little as he said it, radiant energy coming off him like rays of the sun.

For reasons of his own her father had taken to Philip.

Philip always took good care to be very respectful around her father. Brock was someone else again, proud and spirited. He would never play-act a deference he didn't feel. Philip, on the other hand was the definitive "yes" man.

There had always been a lot of drama around Brock Tyson. Lots of sparks. Brock, unlike Philip, had always been ready for anything, but—as the whole community had acknowledged—full of generous emotions. Certainly her father, a hot-hearted man for all his griefs, had had a fierce dislike of Rex Kingsley and his brutal ways with his high-mettled, headstrong grandson.

Shelley knew in her bones she would be in terrible trouble if she ever allowed herself to fall in love with Brock. It would be as easy to tame him as tame an eagle.

She was halfway through unloading the vehicle when Amanda, shoeless, and in a pretty pink ruffled sundress she'd made herself, appeared on the verandah.

"Home again, are you?" she called blithely, leaning on the wrought-iron balustrade. "Good trip?"

"You're joking! It was as hot as Hades, bouncing over the tracks."

"Someone's got to do it," Amanda said breezily. "But I finished up those letters you asked me to do."

"Thank you." Shelley's tone was dry. "They must have taken a long time." Maybe twenty minutes.

"Aren't you a good little girl, doing all that yourself?" Amanda observed, quite willing for Shelley to have all the credit.

"Why don't you give me a hand?" Shelley hung a few bags over her hand and walked up the short flight of steps to the wide verandah, with its planter chairs set at intervals.

"Later." Amanda waved, drained by the heat. She flopped into a chair. "Let's have a little talk first. Gosh, isn't it hot? I don't suppose you brought back any diet cola?"

"I did, as a matter of fact. Especially for you." Shelley deposited her last load.

"Gee, thanks."

"Don't expect me to haul it up for you."

"Dad will do it when he returns," Amanda said carelessly.

"Where is he?"

"Shifting some of the cattle. Now…first things first. Your boyfriend was onto us first thing this morning. He had a very interesting tale to tell."

"Who's my boyfriend supposed to be?" Shelley asked, already knowing the answer. The whole family had been pushing her friendship with Philip Kingsley. If it came to anything it would make things easier for them appeared to be the reasoning.

"Ho-ho, little joke. Phil, of course. If you take my advice—"

"I won't."

"Don't let him get away. Just how many guys are filthy rich *and* good-looking and, more importantly, interested in you?"

"I could name a few wealthy men around here." Shelley started to reel off some names.

"Most of 'em are married." Amanda groaned, thinking she would never get over Mitch Claydon, who had recently wed his childhood sweetheart, Christine Reardon. Okay, Christine was beautiful, but she was six feet tall. At five-six Amanda considered herself just right.

Exhausted, Shelley fell into a rattan armchair opposite her sister, fanning herself vigorously with her cream akubra. "And what did dear Philip have to say?"

Amanda took her time to answer, her eyes focused on her sister's face. After a lifetime she still didn't understand how her sister retained that perfectly beautiful skin while she, a honey-blonde, was always smothering her face in sunblock. Even so she couldn't prevent the tiny coating of freckles across her nose. It just wasn't fair.

"So Brock Tyson is back?" Amanda gave her sister a sharp, searching look.

"His grandfather wanted him home," Shelley said quietly, hoping she hadn't blushed at the mere mention of his name.

"Then Mr Kingsley must be dying?" Amanda didn't sound upset.

"Didn't Philip tell you that?"

"No way! He just said his grandfather wasn't enjoying his usual good health."

"Why doesn't he say things the way they are? That's Philip and his mother all over. They're so secretive it's a little paranoid. Rex Kingsley is dying."

"All right. No need to get huffy. The really big surprise was that you actually had dinner with Brock!"

"So I did." Shelley had a job keeping her tone normal.

"Anything else?" Amanda stared at her.

"What's that supposed to mean?"

Amanda gave a derisive snort. "I'm your sister, remember? At sixteen you had a giant crush on Brock Tyson."

"I wasn't the only one. He was and remains fascinating."

"But trouble. He just threw all his chances away."

"What chances? He's Kingsley's grandson, for God's sake. Surely that means something—blood?"

"Not to that old tyrant. He's dreadful. The male counterpart to the late Mrs Ruth McQueen, God rest her troubled soul. I bet she's queening it over Hades. These old patriarchs and matriarchs! They had too much land. Too much power. Too much money. It must be true that power corrupts. What's Brock look like these days? Wasn't he sexy?"

"I wouldn't worry about whether he's lost any of it," Shelley said dryly. "He was always very handsome, very bold. Nowadays he has a real presence about him."

"Let's call it arrogance. I remember him as arrogant." And he'd never taken any notice of Amanda, which rubbed salt into her wounded ego.

"Maybe. He's certainly very self-assured, with those remarkable light eyes."

"They must be a legacy from the runaway dad," Amanda

commented. "No wonder old Kingsley hates him. Every time he looks at Brock it must remind him of the father."

"Probably," Shelley conceded. "Yet Brock has a look of his grandfather. The chiselled features, the height. Rex Kingsley is a very imposing-looking man."

"But dreadful. So that's it? You had dinner?" Amanda leaned over and seized her younger sister's hand.

"What were you expecting? An orgy?" For such an indolent young woman Amanda had a bone-cracking grip.

"Not with you!" Amanda gave a patronising curl of the lip. "All the guys know you don't put out."

"Whereas you do. You've got yourself a bit of a reputation there, Mandy." Shelley sighed.

"Don't be so sanctimonious," Amanda snapped. "I'm not worried about that at all."

"Maybe you ought to be." Shelley shrugged.

"You just had to say that, didn't you?" The colour in Amanda's pink cheeks darkened.

"I care about you, Mandy. You're my sister. It might be better if you played a little harder to get."

"You're saying that because Mitch Claydon dumped me." Her whole body burned with the terrible memory of the day Mitch had told her in no uncertain terms to get lost.

"He didn't dump you, Amanda," Shelley said, hoping her sister would think straight. "You should stop talking like that. Mitch was never serious about you. There's only one woman in his life and that's Christine. She's a lovely person. She's my friend."

"Puh-lease!" Amanda groaned, touching her temple as though the pain there was excruciating. "Say no more about her. I've already forgotten about Mitch Claydon."

"That's good to know, now he's married."

"When will you see Brock again?" Amanda frowned. She appeared to be tossing up ideas in her head. Shelley could almost see them simmering. "If he's sticking around I might turn my attention to him. You've got Philip safely hooked. It's about time I settled down. I'm the wrong side of twenty-five. I'm pretty, I'm bright, I'm talented." A faint look of torment was on her face.

"Don't worry, Mandy," Shelley suggested, suddenly sorry for her sister. "The right man will come along. You just have to take it easier. But please don't go around telling people Philip and I are an item. We're not. I don't want to mislead people, least of all Philip, and you're a great one for spreading gossip." She should have said making mischief. Amanda was stuck with that label as well.

"Listen, do you want to enjoy the finer things of life, or are you dead set on killing yourself with work?" Amanda retaliated. "Mum and Dad are going to grieve for Sean forever. You could die of hard work and they wouldn't pay any attention. Why don't you listen, you silly girl? If Philip Kingsley asks you to marry him—and you could get him to if you gave him a bit more encouragement—say yes. Yes, yes, *yes*. At least he gives a damn about you. It would be better for the family as well. I know a few guys are interested in you, but Phil's your best option. Keep playing hard to get and he might start looking at someone else."

"He's welcome to," Shelley said. "I might be trying to help my family at the moment, but I'm not going to commit suicide for you. Getting mixed up with Philip and Frances would be as good as killing myself."

"How melodramatic!" Amanda pulled a face.

"I don't think so. People can make very bad decisions in life that have serious consequences. Marrying for love is one thing, even if at some stage the love runs out, but marrying for convenience would do me and my self-esteem a lasting injury. One can't love to order, Mandy."

"Oh, grow up!" Amanda cried in frustration, finding her sister and her principles extreme. "You don't have to be in love with him to make a go of it." Amanda frowned at the burning blue sky. "That's not the important thing when you're considering a good marriage. What a woman looks for is security. A guy who's going to look after her, provide her with the good things in life. It's better that Philip cares more about you than you care for him. It gives a girl bar-gaining power. Besides, Phil's a nice guy. Okay, he's a bit intense but he's good-looking—or he would be if he'd straighten his shoulders and lift his head. Spunky little you could make him do that. If Old Man Kingsley is dying Philip is ready to step into his shoes.''

''You don't really believe that, do you?'' Shelley was starting to feel troubled by the conversation. She really wasn't comfortable with this family push towards Philip, though she'd gone along with the friendship because it had seemed to please her parents.

''What I meant was Philip will inherit,'' Amanda ex-plained patiently, confirming Shelley's fears. ''Do you re-alize what that means? He'll come into a fortune.''

Shelley shook her glowing head. In the heat damp little tendrils were clinging to her cheeks and forehead, giving her the look of a cherub always associated with the Logan twins. ''Philip will never run Kingsley Holdings,'' Shelley said. ''He works very hard, I know, but he doesn't seem to have it in him to get results. He's not a natural-born leader. He's not good with the men. I'm better myself with our own staff. Our little team pulls together and it's mostly for me. Philip lacks authority. The trouble is he's never been his own man.''

''So what?'' Amanda looked at her sister in disgust. ''It's money we're talking about. Position. That homestead. It's still pretty grand but run down. Frances has never been al-lowed to touch it, but you could. We're both very artistic. Phil can hire people—an overseer, manager—who could do all the work.''

''He has his cousin Brock,'' Shelley said simply. ''Brock is family. He too is a grandson.''

Amanda gave her a long, knowing look. ''You don't re-ally believe Kingsley will set Brock above Philip? Philip is the elder, and he's the one who stayed. If everything we've heard is correct Brock's not going to get a razoo.''

Shelley drank in the heavy scent of frangipani from the

garden. "One wonders why his grandfather got him home, then?"

For a moment the sisters regarded one another in silence. "One wonders why he came?" Amanda said finally.

"Why not? When it comes right down to it a lot of Brockway money was poured into Kingsley Holdings. Don't we all believe—and the facts bear it out—that Rex Kingsley talked his wife into handing over all her money?"

"Why wouldn't he?" Sarcasm from Amanda. "He's a truly greedy, manipulative man."

"Brock has Brockway blood in his veins," Shelley reminded her. "His grandmother adored him, but then she had to go and die."

"Perhaps she was glad to." Amanda laughed cynically. "I wouldn't want to be in Rex Kingsley's shoes right now. There's a final reckoning."

"I believe there is," Shelley said quietly. "Brock has been treated very badly. Philip told you about his mother?"

Amanda flapped at an insect buzzing around her buttery curls. "That she died?"

"Poor woman! She didn't have much of a life."

"And whose fault was that?" Amanda suddenly challenged, oddly agitated. "You've got to want things out of life. You've got to have goals and go after them. You can't get yourself stuck in the bloody bush. Why did she and her husband return to Mulgaree? Okay, so she went back to her father, but she must have known what to expect."

"She had a baby and no money, Amanda. She was young, more vulnerable than most, given how she was reared. The princess who was never let out of the castle. Kingsley saw to that."

"She had a husband," Amanda countered.

"I can't answer that question, Mandy. The poor woman is dead. But Brock is here once more, and he's the man for the job."

"God, you'd better not let Philip or his mother hear you say that," Amanda warned, hitching the skirt of her sundress over her pretty knees. "You hardly know Brock anyway. I know him better than you do. You were just a kid when he left. You really should have invited him over, but I suppose it didn't occur to you? Too harried with the shopping?"

"As a matter of fact, I did."

"What?" Amanda sat bolt upright. "What did he say?"

"He said he'd come."

"That's absolutely great!" Amanda's pert face lit up, blue eyes asparkle. "Just occasionally you do something right. I used to think going back a way that Brock was kind of interested in me."

"You were interested in him, more likely." Shelley corrected, a little more tartly than she'd intended. Brock and Amanda? No, no, no!

"Well, he wasn't interested in you, that's for sure," Amanda responded, pouring on the acid. "What will happen when Phil finds out that you've got a soft spot for Brock? You'd be a real fool to jeopardize your relationship. Especially now, when he's right on the brink of his reward. You'd better tell him Brock's coming over to see *me*. He'll accept that. I'm very popular with the guys." She adjusted the strap of her pink sundress, cut low in front and undeniably sexy.

"Maybe I'd better leave it to you to tell Dad that I've invited Brock," Shelley said. "He accepts things much better from you."

"No problem. Dad loves me. I'm his firstborn." Amanda, as usual, was quite complacent about the open favouritism. She looked flushed, unable to suppress the sudden burst of excitement. "Besides, for all we know Brock might fall passionately in love with me."

"I'll be amazed if he does," Shelley said dryly.

"You should try to deal with your jealousy, Shel. I hate it when you get like that."

"I'm just being realistic," Shelley warned. "I don't know that you're Brock's type, Mandy."

"He's a man, isn't he?" Amanda drawled, lacing her fingers and then stretching her arms above her head with voluptuous grace. "So we didn't hit it off in the old days? I've had quite a bit of experience since then. If Brock somehow gets himself back into Kingsley's good graces, in particular back into his will, then that will make all the difference in the world. We'll know I've found the right man to go after." Amanda laid a cool hand on top of her sister's. "You know, Shel, this sounds strangely like fate."

Shelley realized with a jolt that her sister was serious.

Here we go again, she thought. If and whenever Brock took time to visit, one thing was certain: Amanda was going to come on real strong. Fantasy fulfilment was Amanda's thing. For once in her life Shelley wasn't sure she could watch it.

Brock's grandfather lay in the massive oak bed, his once towering frame oddly slight beneath the tight coverings on the bed. It gave him no joy to witness this shocking deterioration. Like his cousin, he didn't care to see his larger-than-life grandfather so diminished. Even the stern, handsome face had changed. It had lost its forbidding expression. Despite the sudden sparseness, the matting of his pewter-coloured hair, the pronounced pallor and the deep grooves that ran from nose to mouth and down the chin, Rex Kingsley looked at peace with himself and his past.

A nurse in a white uniform sat composedly beside his bed, ankles touching, hands folded neatly in her lap. She was middle-aged and competent-looking, with narrow glasses perched on her nose.

"Oh, it's you, Mr Tyson," she said, looking up, her face brightening.

"How is he?" he asked quietly.

"Not good today. But he's been hoping to see you."

"Thank you, Nurse. I'll sit with him for a while. You can take a break."

"Is there something I can get you?" she asked, almost whispering. "Tea, coffee?"

"Nothing. I'm fine." He gave her a smile.

"I won't be far away." Colour rose in her cheeks.

"Thank you." He took her place in the chair beside his grandfather's extraordinary Victorian bed. It was Gothic in style, the rich claret-coloured hangings held in place by sumptuous tasselled tie-backs. This was the bed he'd die in for sure.

Things would change dramatically with his grandfather gone. Philip's mother, Frances, was already pushing herself forward as the mistress of Mulgaree, as mother to the heir apparent.

Oh, my God, what am I doing here? Brock thought, half covering his face with his hand. He hated this man. Not so much for what he had done to him, but to his mother. Why were you so cruel to her? Given you loved her once, why did you turn on her? For loving my father, a man you apparently despised?

Yet his mother had always insisted his father had been anything but a weak man. On the contrary, he'd felt outraged and angry trapped at Mulgaree. The only thing that had kept him there was the strength of his love for her and for his child.

What price had he paid?

He'd always believed his grandfather had been mixed up in his father's disappearance. There were layers and layers of treachery and cunning behind that grey near-sepulchral face on the pillow. How else could he have inflicted endless bullying on people he was supposed to care about? Finally, without quite knowing how, Philip and Frances had managed to turn Kingsley against them completely and they'd been out. Banished.

Now he knew it had really been an escape. He and his mother had retreated from an unwinnable battle. Yet his mother had always maintained "You are the future of Mulgaree, my darling. The power will be yours."

He could hear her voice resonate in his head. So easy to believe it when love and reverence for the land ran through his blood. It was the one thing about him the old man had been able to understand.

My grandfather. My enemy. Why should I trust him to rewrite his will?

"I'll be looking out for you" was the last thing his mother had said. He wondered if anyone who passed over to the other side really could.

He wondered about Shelley Logan, who had offered him two things last night. An extraordinary relief from grief and a much too dangerous excitement. Shelley knew too much about pain for him to wish to hurt her further. And hurt her he would if he took over his grandfather's mantle.

Maybe he even had some of Kingsley's ruthlessness in him? Maybe he would take on some of Kingsley's personality if he stepped into the role? The years he'd been away from his grandfather and Mulgaree he'd had a good image of himself. Important people he'd admired had depended on him, trusted him. He had made many friends.

But now he was back and the old darkness had descended so quickly.

There was so much trauma surrounding the old man. Yet he knew which grandson must win if it came to a fight to inherit. Who had the stamina, the superior strength. Who could hold what he had built up together. It wasn't benevolence or contrition that had caused Kingsley to beg him to come home. It was the fear his dream might come to an end in the wrong hands. No matter how much he might loathe Brock, he needed him to govern his empire after his death. And now that he had him home Kingsley was going to die happy in the knowledge that his name and his life's work would survive. It was one of life's serious riddles how even the worst never dared go against blood.

Brock took his hand away from his head, suddenly realizing with a shock that his grandfather was staring at him.

"Who are you?" his grandfather demanded hoarsely. "Get away from me."

His face was so stricken Brock couldn't control an instinctive pity. "I'm your grandson. You wanted me home, remember? Look long and hard. It's Brock."

Kingsley continued to stare at him as if he were his mortal enemy. "Stay away!" he cried, looking terrified. "Get back."

Brock released an explosion of breath, instantly rising to his feet. "Calm yourself, old man. I'm going." It was obviously the painkilling drugs disturbing Kingsley's mind.

"Let me die in peace."

Was it possible that tears squeezed out of the old man's eyes? "I won't bother you." Brock, who worried he had a chunk of the old man in him, responded to the anguish. His grandfather looked already dead. "I'll send your nurse back."

The sigh from the bed was like a death rattle. "I destroyed you." For a moment Kingsley was lucid.

"Is that it?" Brock turned back to demand. "You mean to cut me out? Is that why you brought me back here? To continue our rift?"

"Where is my daughter? Where is Catherine?" Now Kingsley's face was alight with feverish anxiety.

"She's dead," Brock answered harshly, trying to calm himself but tremendously upset at the sound of his mother's name. "Like you soon will be." You killed her, he thought, but he didn't have the cruelty in him to say it. "She's free at last."

"Dear God, Daniel." The voice from the bed now issued so powerfully it caught Brock by surprise.

Rex Kingsley with a supreme effort cleared his brain. He was so full of pain. Pain that seared through his body like a licking, burning trail of fire. It was agonizing. The pain had all but defeated him. Another man would not have survived so long. The drugs that were meant to shut down the poker-hot agony were all but useless after the shortest time.

"Daniel—here. Come back here." He had to end this battle. Buried deep inside him the love for his younger grandson was struggling to find a way out.

"What is it you want?" Brock moved back towards the bed. "You need me, don't you, Grandfather? How can you bear it?"

Astonishingly, Kingsley grabbed his hand, held on as though in human contact the terrible pain could be made bearable. "You were a boy who felt no fear at all. The grandson I always wanted. Not content to live an ordinary life. I knew I loved you."

"Is that what caused you to treat me so badly?" Brock asked with deep bitterness. "Make or break?"

"You were wild." Kingsley held onto his hand, though Brock made an attempt to withdraw it. "I was obliged to. But I was proud of you. Proud of the way you could disappear into thin air. I sent men looking for you, our best aboriginal trackers, but you were one with the desert."

"Maybe they were deliberately looking where they knew they'd never find me," Brock said, knowing a little of that was true. The men had been loyal to Kingsley out of fear. They'd always turned a blind eye to his escapades, essentially on his side.

"I know they tried to protect you, but they had no right. I am your grandfather. I had to do what I thought best. I had to stop you. Bring you back. Your father was a waster."

"You'd do well to get off the subject of my father," Brock said, his voice deep and daunting. "All my life I've thought there was something you could tell me about his disappearance."

"He bolted. Left you and your mother." Kingsley peered at him. "You've got his eyes, you know."

"You don't seem to be able to deal with that."

Kingsley moved his head on the pillow. "Catherine and I were so close. I idolised her. I gave her everything she wanted."

"Except freedom."

"She never loved your father so much she would leave me." There was a strange triumph on the old man's face. "I forebade her to see Tyson. She defied me. Once she would never have contemplated doing such a thing. But I loved her."

"And now you're looking for forgiveness before you stand before your Maker?"

"It's true." Kingsley gave a deathly smile. "A man gets like that when the arrival of the Grim Reaper is imminent."

"I wish I could say I forgive you, but I don't, Grandfather. That kind of forgiveness died with my mother."

"But she's here right now," the old man said, suddenly pointing into the shadows at the far end of the darkened room.

Such was the conviction in his grandfather's voice that for a minute Brock almost turned his head. But that way lay madness. The old man was hallucinating. "No, she's lost to you forever."

"She's standing just behind your shoulder." Kingsley's eyes filled up. "I've made my peace with her."

"And with the others? Philip and Frances? What of them? They won't let go. You've allowed Philip to believe he's your heir."

"They've been taken care of," Kingsley rasped, his shaky hand moving dismissively. "You have my promise, as I told you. Mulgaree belongs to you. The world I created, it's yours for life. After that it passes to your son—Catherine's grandchild."

"Does that make you feel much better?" This was atonement, plain and simple.

"It was meant to be, Daniel. I gambled on Philip, but the idea of Philip taking over is too dreadful to allow. I rarely make mistakes, but I did with him. He doesn't have the steel."

"Why are you so sure I have?" Brock stared into his

grandfather's eyes, the pupils greatly enlarged from the drugs.

"You survived it all. You're tough. That's important. You need to be in a man's world. You're fit to be the living symbol of Kingsley Holdings. Therefore I want you to change your name by deed poll to Kingsley. You're Daniel Brockway Kingsley—understand?"

"You want me to renounce my father?"

"He was never a father to you," Kingsley reminded him harshly. "I reared you and your cousin. I kept Catherine and Frances secure and comfortable. They wanted for nothing."

Except love and acceptance from a man with a heart of lead.

CHAPTER FOUR

THE end wasn't to come easy. Rex Kingsley was to be punished. He passed a desperate night when he actually started to pray that the Lord—if there was one—would take him. With the big things in life Rex Kingsley had always been prepared to gamble.

The nurse gave him another shot of morphine at dawn. She was astounded her patient had managed to live through the early hours of the morning, when many a suffering soul was released. But somehow Rex Kingsley managed to hold on, even though there were periods when he blacked out with the pain.

The answer was simple. A will of iron ran through him, a sense of purpose often put to ruthless use but utterly genuine.

The nurse had been told Mr Kingsley's solicitor, Gerald Maitland of Maitland-Pearson, a big legal firm in the State capital, Brisbane, was flying in the following day. The solicitor had already made the hellishly long trip, weeks before; now Rex Kingsley was dragging him back.

Frances Kingsley, a striking brunette in her mid-fifties, but looking nowhere near that age, believed it signalled bad news for her and her son.

"What do you suppose is happening?" she asked with equal parts of fear and frustration. "Has Brock managed to worm his way back into your grandfather's good graces?"

Philip grimaced. "I wouldn't associate Brock with worms," he said grimly, the jealousy in his voice more chilling than his mother's open anger.

"He can't take precedence over you," Frances protested strongly, knowing how Philip as a boy had yearned to be like his cousin. "You're the elder. You've been here all the time. We stuck it out."

"My God, haven't we?" Philip said, bitterness taking control of him. "You don't think it significant Grandfather wanted Brock to sit with him last night?"

"That's not love," Frances scoffed, desperate to believe it. "That's the old man trying to gain forgiveness. He might have lived as though he was far above the rest of us but he's not the equal of God. You can bet your life Rex Kingsley has many stains on his soul."

Philip laughed discordantly. "We've got a few ourselves." He struggled with his sense of guilt, made stronger since he'd come to know of his aunt Catherine's premature death.

"I won't discuss them, Philip!" Frances burst out, her face cold. "I did what I had to do to secure Mulgaree for you."

"I know that." Philip bowed his head. "But it was unjust, Mother. The lies you told about Brock. And Aunt Catherine. She was always so nice to me, but you were awful to Brock. I'm sorry Aunt Catherine's dead. It shouldn't have happened. And so far away! I'm sorry about a lot of things. All those lies! It was like goading a bull."

"At any rate the bull believed them," his mother answered with shameless sarcasm. "You'll be a lot sorrier if somehow your cousin manages to cut you out—literally at the death."

"We just have to pray to God, Mother, that he doesn't," Philip said, desperate for his inheritance but intimidated by all that went with it.

He could never step into his grandfather's shoes. Never! On the other hand he could see Brock taking over the reins. Even at his wildest Brock had commanded affection from the men, and a certain wry respect. Especially after Brock had turned his grandfather's beatings against him. He still had the sight of his beaten grandfather, shocked senseless, imprinted on his mind.

"I suppose we could put a stop to it," Frances said very slowly, not meeting her son's dismayed eyes.

"I'll ignore that, Mother. Grandfather might be on his deathbed but I'd never underestimate him or his faculties, or even think of perhaps hurrying things along. His nurse rarely leaves his side."

"As if I couldn't handle that woman." Frances thrust a hand through her dark hair, which she continued to wear in a perfect side-parted pageboy. "You're the one underestimating the urgency—"

"Of what?"

Brock startled them greatly by suddenly appearing in the room. A tiger couldn't have trodden more noiselessly, Philip thought, wondering how much his cousin had heard.

As it happened, nothing save the last remark. But Brock caught a flicker of something like fear in Frances's dark eyes.

She smiled icily. "You should pay more attention to your manners, Brock. You never did have any. This is a private conversation."

"Obviously about Grandfather." Brock barely concealed his contempt for her. His mother's enemy.

Philip glared at him. "Grandfather, is he now? He was always the old man or Kingsley."

"Careful of what you say, Phil," Brock drawled, fixing his shining gaze on his cousin. "In fact, you ought to be careful about everything."

"I...don't know what you mean."

"Of course you do," Brock replied dangerously.

Frances shifted her chair out of a strong ray of sunlight that fell into Rex Kingsley's huge dark-panelled study, with its scores of books, mostly non-fiction, filling the shelves from floor to ceiling, its pageantry of blue ribbons for prize-winning stock, gleaming trophies, the collector's treasure trove of guns in a locked glass-fronted cabinet.

"What is it you want, Brock?" she asked angrily.

"Don't get ahead of yourself, Frances," he warned. "Ac--

tually, it's my business, not yours. But I don't mind if you know. I want the keys for the helicopter. I have a little trip in mind.''

Philip, who had been sitting crouched in a rich claret-coloured leather armchair, shot to his feet. ''Well, you darned well can't have it!'' Colour rose alarmingly beneath his tanned skin.

''Dear me!'' Brock glanced at his cousin as though he fully expected his reaction. ''It's already been cleared with the old man.''

''I don't believe this. Since when did you learn to fly a helicopter?'' Philip made it sound insurmountably difficult.

''You think I'd try without a licence? It'd be safer to walk. Relax, Phil. I have notched up five thousand hours on a helicopter in Ireland. I regularly flew my boss and his friends and colleagues across to England and France.''

''How clever you are, Brock,'' Frances sneered. There had never been anything the boy couldn't do. Now he was a man. That meant big trouble. Brock was clever. He understood ambition even if he had got into the absurd habit of putting his mother's wellbeing before his own. Now Catherine was gone and Brock's ambitions had free rein.

''This helicopter is a completely different machine,'' Philip muttered, taking a few steps towards a long rack behind the massive partner's desk that held many bunches of keys, all clearly labelled.

''I can handle it,'' Brock said in a level voice, blocking his cousin's way. He was taller, heavier, superbly fit and looking it.

''So where are you taking it?'' Philip challenged, giving in reluctantly, inevitably, as he always had with Brock.

''Over to Wybourne. I told Shelley I'd like to look in on her tourist operation.''

''Shelley?'' Philip almost yelled in a great surge of emotion. ''Shelley's *mine*!'' he insisted, like a petulant child.

''Wishful thinking, pal.'' Brock's tone was quiet, a touch contemptuous.

"Stop this now, Philip," Frances thundered, looking wrathfully at her son, who was standing there gritting his teeth. "The Logans are nobodies. Absolute nobodies. They tell me Paddy Logan has turned into a heavy drinker. The mother stays in her room all day, and the elder girl, Amanda, is little more than a slut. As for Shelley—"

"You can't sling any mud at Shelley!" Philip dared to give his mother a nakedly hostile stare. "She's beautiful. She's good and sweet and smart."

"I'd almost forgotten you had a decent streak in you, Phil." Brock gave his cousin a half-mocking, half-sympathetic smile. "You're right about Shelley. She's a saint. In fact, she's damned near perfect."

"You keep your hands off her," Philip warned, hazel eyes flashing. "She's my girl. When the time comes I'm going to ask her to marry me."

"Over my dead body!" Frances cut in violently. "There's a huge gap between the Logans and us. All right, I apologise about Shelley, but she's the only member of her family one could invite to the house."

"God, Mother, you're such a snob!" Philip exclaimed, looking as if he was on the verge of crying.

"With no real basis for your snobbery," Brock said. "Aren't I right in thinking Grandfather believed Uncle Aaron married beneath him?"

Frances turned a bright shade of crimson. "How dare you, Brock? My family is perfectly respectable. I won't hear a word against them. I didn't shock them by running off with a penniless adventurer, like your precious mother."

"Of whom you were excessively jealous. How my father's memory has been tarnished," Brock said. "But he wasn't a Judas, which is more than I can truly say for you, Frances. Now, pleasantries over—you must excuse me." Brock reached out a long arm for the keys to the helicopter.

"You could have told me. I could have taken you," Philip said unexpectedly.

"Come, if you like."

Philip's face reflected his shock. "You're serious?"

"I never waste time saying things I don't mean." In fact it was Shelley who'd suggested it. Probably at pains to put him in his place, he thought with bleak amusement.

Frances closed her eyes as if in pain. When she opened them she glared at her son. "I forbid you to go, Philip. Your place is here. Grandfather could slip away in your absence."

"He'd better not," Brock said with the faintest touch of menace. "Grandfather won't go until he has straightened out his affairs. He's waiting for Gerald Maitland to arrive. Good old Gerald! The two of you still good friends, Frances?" Brock fixed her with cynical eyes.

Frances, already wary, was suddenly afraid of him. "I have no idea what you're getting at, Brock." But her olive skin had reddened. "I've known Gerald for many years. I was at his wife's funeral. She passed away almost two years ago." She stared back at him with loathing. "Philip will inherit. Make no mistake."

"Have you ever thought Phil mightn't want the job?" Brock asked. "Take time off to think about it, Frances. We'll be back late afternoon, I expect."

Brock set the chopper down on the large front lawn of the Wybourne homestead.

"You shouldn't have done that!" Philip remonstrated. "Mr Logan won't like it—not to mention the noise of the rotor!"

Brock, being Brock, ignored him. "Might wake him up," he replied harshly.

Amanda was waiting for them, waving prettily from the verandah, but her bright blue eyes were focused entirely on Brock.

Gosh, what a sexy walk, she thought, unable to take her eyes off him. A few steps behind was Philip, his slight stoop made more noticeable by comparison with his cousin's head up, shoulders back stance, and that lithe, cat-like co-ordination. She was pleased Philip had tagged along. Now

he could team up with Shelley while she was free to con-
centrate on Brock, who appeared more gorgeous than ever.

With both young men now joining her, Amanda reached
up and threw her arms effusively around Brock's neck, kissing his cheek as if they'd once been the greatest of friends.

"Welcome back, Brock! I'm absolutely thrilled you've
come to visit." She spared Philip a sideways glance.
"How's it going, Phil?" Phil always looked as if he was
carrying the weight of the world on his shoulders. God, he
was a bore! He always looked depressed.

"I've had better times. Grandfather is failing fast."

"I'm so sorry," said Amanda, managing to sound sympathetic when in fact she was busy thinking the sooner the
better.

"Where's Shelley?" Brock asked, wondering how he
could prise Amanda's pretty white hand off his arm without
actually detaching her fingers one by one. He glanced over
his shoulder into the dim interior of the house. It didn't look
cool. It looked gloomy. Or maybe that was the pervading
atmosphere.

"She'll be here shortly," Amanda said, her pleasure going a little sour at the expression on Brock's face. "She's
getting lunch ready." She indicated an area on the verandah
with a long table set attractively for *al fresco* dining.

"Maybe you should go and help her?" Brock suggested
with a mocking smile. "We'll sit here, if we may." He
moved back to a planter's chair. "Are we to have the pleasure of saying hello to your father and mother? It's a very
long time since I've seen them."

"Actually, Brock, Dad has taken Mum into Koomera
Crossing," Amanda lied, like a true professional. Which in
many ways she was. Her father had a serious hangover—
he would surely die of cirrhosis of the liver—and her mother
was too darn neurotic to make an appearance. "Mum has
an appointment with Dr Sarah. They'll stay overnight at the
pub."

"Maybe next time," Brock said, his keen antennae sensing he wasn't being given the truth.

Some fragrance floated past him, like a burst of orange blossom. He turned his head expectantly as Shelley found her way out onto the verandah.

"Sorry I wasn't here to greet you!" She tried to suppress her excitement, flashing a smile at both cousins, her smile impartial. She thought it best to keep her attraction to Brock well hidden for a good number of reasons—including self-preservation. She didn't want to make trouble for him either, especially not now, when his grandfather was dying and there was so much resentment at Mulgaree. "I heard the chopper."

"Who wouldn't?" Philip grumbled, putting a possessive hand on her arm. "I'm sorry. I told Brock not to land there." He made it sound as if Brock was a rank amateur. "Thank goodness your father and mother aren't at home."

"Actually, it's a good idea," Shelley answered, avoiding having to repeat the lie. "It's foolish to land too far away. You always have too big a hike to the house, Philip. It's not as though we don't have plenty of room."

She gestured to the great open space in front of the homestead, the broad acres of grass, sun-scorched to a bright apricot, a scattering of majestic date palms, stands of grey and blue gum trees, blazing shrubbery that could withstand the dry heat and massive indifference. It was now hard to believe that her mother, in the early days of her marriage, had been devoted to the task of keeping a large area of dry climate garden and a vegetable patch alive.

"We didn't want to put you to the trouble of making lunch." Brock looked straight into Shelley's emerald eyes, pinning her in place.

What was happening with this girl was too swift, he thought with sudden disquiet. He had a powerful impulse to kiss her again. Not her cheek, but her mouth. He could still feel it trembling under his. Shelley Logan's effect on him was far more radical than he could allow. He'd long trained himself to be self-sufficient, but now he found the sight of this little Outback girl as fascinating as finding a delicately petalled wildflower in a rock crevice.

She wore a pink shirt with tiny pearly buttons over her jeans, and if anyone thought a redhead shouldn't wear pink they should think again—or maybe Shelley's beautiful skin changed the rules.

"It's no trouble at all." Shelley appeared bright and friendly, despite the turbulent feelings that were sweeping through her. Fronting up to Brock again took every ounce of her poise and self-confidence. "It's all ready."

"Isn't there something I can do to help?" Brock enquired. Why the heck had he brought Philip? he asked himself angrily. Unless to protect her...

From himself.

He wasn't a harmless kind of guy. There was such a torrent dammed up inside him that it wouldn't make life easy for any woman, let alone an innocent like Shelley.

Philip pushed away from the wrought-iron balustrade. "Let me," he said eagerly. "You stay here and talk to Amanda."

"We'll have plenty of time for that." Brock took charge, smoothly turning Shelley in the direction of the hall. "I came over to talk about this Outback Adventures operation, remember? Who knows? I might decide to run one myself."

Amanda, offended, nevertheless decided to follow. Only Philip, hot and thirsty, chose that precise moment to request a drink. He could see a big glass jug, frosty with condensation, which he knew would be full of Shelley's excellent home-made lemonade, with slices of lemon floating in it and tiny sprigs of mint.

"So, Amanda, what have you been doing with yourself since I saw you last?" he asked, with a determined effort to be sociable though he didn't like Amanda at all.

He settled his long length into a planter's chair, moving another companionably closer. Was there nothing he could do to beat Brock to the jump? Brock not only didn't obey the rules, he didn't even know them. His grandfather behaved in the same way...

In the kitchen, bright and attractive given the dullness and relative sparseness of the rest of the house, Brock leaned against the sink and watched Shelley moving about. She didn't appear the least bit self-conscious under his gaze. Those blazing kisses might never have happened.

But then he saw her outstretched hand faintly tremble. Deep inside her she was throwing out a challenge. He admired that. She moved swiftly and gracefully, at ease if not with him with what she was doing.

"That was an excuse, wasn't it?" she asked, looking up at him. "You don't want to know about my tourist scheme?"

He shook his head. "Of course I do. I respect resourceful people who know how to make a go of things."

"But you've absolutely no intention of doing something like it yourself?"

He eased away from the flood of sunlight coming in the large window. Sunlight that drew plum-coloured highlights from his raven hair. "I wouldn't have the time. Running the Kingsley empire will be a full-time job."

"Are things already determined?" she asked.

"What do you mean?"

"Has your grandfather said something positive to you?" In her urgency she came so close to him they were almost touching.

"None of your business, Miss Shelley."

"I'm sorry." She flushed under his brilliant gaze.

A long lock of her beautiful hair had fallen out of its upswept arrangement, provoking him to reach out and hook it behind her ear. For all her attempts at calmness and detachment he was very conscious that the attraction between them would take very little to ignite. His hand, tanned and bronzed against her white skin, brushed her cheek. It was a brief almost accidental contact that turned suddenly electric.

"Remember your vows." Suddenly challenge sparkled out of her green eyes.

"Damned near impossible around you," he grunted, clamping down on a rush of desire.

"I can see you're a man who loves women."

"I certainly loved my mother."

"I know, Brock." She turned away.

"I think you do. The thing is, my grandfather is not a man I can trust, Shelley. He's a devil, a twister and a tormentor. He's a man living in a world of his own making. The only thing I can trust is the fact he wouldn't want his world destroyed."

"That doesn't say much for poor Philip." Sympathy gathered around her eyes.

"I guess it doesn't." Brock gave her a brooding stare.

"He's worked so hard. Suffered so much humiliation at his grandfather's hands. I know what straining to please is like."

"Stop acting like Philip is precious to you," he said with a decided edge.

"What can it possibly mean to you, Brock? Anyone would feel sorry for him."

"Not me, Shelley girl."

"Then why did you bring him?" she asked, thoroughly puzzled. "I know I suggested it, but I didn't think you would."

"Are you disappointed or pleased?" He watched her, narrow-eyed. "Actually, I had no intention of asking him right up until the last minute. But strategy dictated I keep him right under my nose."

"Strategy?" For some reason she winced. "Of course you'd have a strategy. In a way you're almost as imperious as your grandfather."

A flash like lightning came from his remarkable eyes. "Don't say that, even in fun. For your information, I hardly make a move without a strategy, so don't go judging me."

She was unrepentant. "Far from judging you, I'm on your

side. At least, I think I am. Though obviously you're not overwhelmingly friendly today, I don't want to see you get hurt or cause hurt, Brock. Which I know you're capable of. Like exacting revenge, for instance, for the way you and your mother were treated. It might rebound on you. Eat away at your soul. Besides, Philip's not the problem. He's very much influenced by his mother.''

Brock permitted himself a cynical sigh. ''Tell me something I don't know.''

''I'll have to grow a new layer of skin around you.''

''Why?'' He held her green eyes.

''Because you're so damned caustic.''

''Which is why you prefer Phil?''

She chose her words carefully. ''At least Philip isn't dangerous to know.''

He laughed grimly. ''I feel duty-bound to tell you that you don't know Philip as well as you think you do. There's obsessiveness in his nature. It's not ardour. And don't forget,'' Brock continued arrogantly, ''you loved being kissed by me.''

''Hah!'' Shelley almost leapt away. ''You're excessively sure of yourself, aren't you?''

''Put it this way. I've learned a lot about women.''

''That's not lost on me, but I'm not about to burn my fingers.''

''A lot of women need excitement, Shelley. They can't get it fast enough. Charming, worldly women, bored to distraction.''

''Are you telling me you helped out?''

''Absolutely!'' he mocked. ''I needed to get a whole lot out of my system.''

''And you're still not cured?''

''I didn't expect the girl next door to turn me on.''

Heat flushed her whole body. ''Just how long do your dalliances with physical attraction last?''

''Well, I'm not over you yet! Go easy, there.''

Flustered, she'd been tearing an iceberg lettuce to near

shreds without realizing it. "I bet a few women have wanted to kill you."

"None that I know of."

"Did you ever come close to falling in love with any one of them?" She dared to glance at him for a moment.

"Why do you want to know?" His brilliant gaze locked on hers.

"Just curious."

"Being in love ain't for me, baby." He laughed and picked up a juicy red apple, biting into it with his fine white teeth.

"Too bad." She reached for a large serving platter that already held a colourful galaxy of green beans, red peppers, spring onions and chillies, lining it with the lettuce. Next she garnished the whole with olives, black and green. Finally she added dressing from a small jug.

"*Voilà!*" he said. "I'm impressed."

"By which part of it?"

His hand came forward to clamp on her wrist. "You're turning into a flirt before my very eyes."

"I am not," she protested. "You enjoy challenging women, Brock Tyson. You always did. Don't forget I remember you from your lordly days, when you played at having all the girls in love with you."

"Rubbish. The charge is quite untrue."

"Charm. Deadly charm," she continued, as though he hadn't spoken. "It works all the time."

"Not on you?" He started to play with her fingers.

"I'm too sensible. Stop that!" She pulled her hand away, feeling quite peculiar.

"You just have occasional flashes of letting your hair down?"

He stood there staring down at her, thumbs in the pockets of his jeans, elegant hands splayed over his lean hips. He looked marvellous, bitter, proud. The most physical man she had ever known. "You can use up some of your abundant energy and carry the food out,'' she said, exasperated but even more thrilled.

"Yes, ma'am. Would you like me to take both platters?'' He indicated thickly sliced cold chicken breasts on a bed of multi-coloured pasta.

"Think you can manage it?''

He gave her a droll look. "Do you know, my mother couldn't cook? She never had to. I don't think she even knew what the inside of a kitchen looked like before we left Mulgaree. Maybe a slight exaggeration, but Grandfather always employed a housekeeper. We always had servants. Eula has been at Mulgaree ever since I can remember.''

"Yes, I know,'' she answered quietly. "I often run into her in the town. She was dreadfully upset when you and your mother left. She must be thrilled you're back?''

He nodded. "Devastated about my mother, however.''

"Of course. She told me she adored her. She's very tight-lipped about Philip's mother.''

"The woman of the iron will.'' He grimaced. "I think we might leave Frances to heaven.''

"Okay.'' Shelley swiftly backtracked in an effort to calm him. "So, you're trying to tell me *you* were the cook?''

"Is that so hard to believe? And take care how you answer.''

"I believe you could do anything you wanted to do, Brock. No problem.''

"What if I told you I want to kiss you this minute,'' he said abruptly, not even bothering to suppress the desire in his eyes. Nothing gentle. But fierce, deep, burning into her flesh. He longed to make love before all love was lost.

Shelley didn't answer at once. Her throat was blocked with emotion. "What good would come of it?'' she managed finally.

"Who knows?'' She was like a flower. A rose. Something natural and lovely. "I'd better shut the hell up,'' he pronounced edgily. The longer he stayed near her the higher his desire would mount.

"I don't want that. I don't want you not to talk to me."
It came out far more emotionally than she'd intended.

"Shelley—!"

But whatever he was going to reply she wasn't to hear.
Both of them were alert to the sound of footsteps tapping
along the polished floor of the hallway.

Amanda.

Shelley tried hard to clear her face of expression.

"I'd never hurt you, Shelley." His voice was rich and
deep, deliberately pitched low.

"It could happen without your trying. You know it. I
know it." In the bright light of day she fancied they were
back in a moonlit night, locked in one another's arms.

"I'm not playing a game with you. Don't think that. This
is my head and heart in conflict. I'd like to change my life,
but I can't. And I won't. My future is in the balance."

Tension stretched between them, so strong that for a moment Shelley felt unable to function—only Amanda appeared in the open doorway, blue eyes flashing from one to
the other.

"What's keeping you two?" she demanded, her voice
loaded with implication. "I thought you said lunch was
ready, Shel?"

Shelley was abruptly re-energised. "All bar the finishing
touches," she replied, amazed her voice sounded near
enough to normal. "I never dress the salad until the very
last moment. Now you're here, Mandy, would you like to
grab the basket of rolls?"

CHAPTER FIVE

IT CAME as no surprise when Amanda and Philip tagged along on the bush trek that Shelley had planned to take Brock on.

Philip had insisted on helping Shelley to clear away, while Amanda finished off an icy light beer with Brock. There was no way Amanda was going to be done out of the opportunity of getting to know Brock Tyson a whole lot better. Something about the way he turned his silver gaze on Shelley alarmed her but Shelley was already taken, she reassured herself.

Philip would make an excellent husband. Rich and sober, he was the highest bidder—already a firm favourite with the family. As for Brock? Men like that knew how to enslave a woman. Plus the fact there was always the possibility Rex Kingsley would reinstate his prodigal grandson in his will. Amanda rather fancied joining the ranks of the idle rich, having been idle, though not necessarily rich, nearly all her life.

Brock drove. It just happened like that. He didn't even bother to use his persuasive power. Shelley sat up front beside him, with Philip and Amanda in the back. Shelley was the navigator, pointing out various spots of particular interest to the station's guests, and Amanda kept interjecting, saying there were better places they could go.

"It's so hot in the back," she complained. "Why don't we find somewhere cool, like Malkie Creek? We should have brought our swimsuits," she purred suggestively.

Amanda looked like an ice-cream, begging to be licked, Brock thought. But did she interest him? No. Though Amanda's blue eyes, meeting his in the rear-vision mirror, were telling him the answer should be, Hell, yes! Evidently she was looking for an affair—except it was her sister who tempted him, without even trying.

The heat of the afternoon was compensated for by the glowing colours of the vast landscape. Every hour of the day had its own colour palette: the rocks, the distant eroded hills and ridges with their weird formations, softened by a larkspur haze, the eternal Spinifex that clothed the harsh, fiery earth gold. They presented the full range of dry ochre colours: flaming red, orange, cinnabar, pink, white and yellow, brown and black. Colours that stood out in bold contrast to the deep blue of the clear skies.

Such was the sweeping flatness of the mulga plains they travelled across, the areas of rock formations, naked of any vegetation, and the chains of giant boulders, taking on the dimensions of towering hills. The country was in drought, so the sun-drenched earth was watertight, iron-hard. The wind-sculptured clay pans were crazed and cracked, encrusted with salt so the yellow sands were bleached white.

"No drought lasts forever," Brock said, reading Shelley's mind.

"We haven't had rain for almost two years," she mourned.

"Pray the skies will open up in a thunderstorm or a tropical cyclone will swing in from the North."

"Then we'll have a flood," Amanda crowed from the back seat.

"Maybe, but wherever flood waters spread a new cycle of life begins for the desert," Brock said. "The response to water is truly stupendous. All those countless millions of newly germinated seeds, spreading like wildfire across the red earth. Anywhere the water has gravitated. I've seen some very beautiful sights over the last few years but nothing that moves me as much as our own Channel Country after rain. Wildflowers to the horizons! A spring to end all springs. Surely paradise couldn't look or smell better. It's the visual extravagance, I suppose. The infiniteness. That incredible desert vastness under an ecstasy of flowering.''

His words burned pleasure deep inside Shelley. ''That sounds lovely, Brock.'' He understood. He felt as she felt, finding great joy and consolation in the timeless landscape. ''I've had the most wonderful times of my life recording varieties of wildflowers,'' she confided, her voice full of her own quiet pleasures.

''Isn't that pathetic?'' Amanda scoffed. ''It must be really bad when your best times are drawing flowers. Anyway, don't get her started. Shel can go on for hours about all the little paper daisies, the desert pea and the desert rose, the pink mulla-mullas and the parakeelya, the Star of Bethlehem and the wild cockscomb, and so forth and so on. It's so boring for the rest of us!''

That went down badly with Philip. ''Shelley is an artist,'' he told Amanda heatedly. ''Her drawings are perfectly beautiful. She should be allowed to follow her talent, not wear herself out trying to make a go of this bloody station.''

''I enjoy it, Philip,'' Shelley corrected him quickly, throwing a quelling glance over her shoulder. ''I've learned a lot.''

''You could learn a lot more if you travelled,'' he sighed. ''Saw something of life. I hate the way you have to work so hard.''

''Then isn't it about time you asked her to marry you?'' Amanda dared him.

''Thank you, Amanda, but that's our business,'' Philip said stiffly.

''Why are neither of you considering Shelley doesn't want to?'' Brock spoke in an even tone, strongly at variance with fury in his eyes.

''Oh, she wants to,'' Amanda said with a playful, provocative grin. ''I guess she tells me so just about seven days a week.''

Even knowing her sister, Shelley was shocked. ''Do me a favour and stick to the truth, Amanda,'' she said sharply, thinking that if it were true Amanda wouldn't have hesitated to betray her trust.

"Oh, look—we've embarrassed her." Amanda turned sideways to poke a resistant Philip in the ribs. "Okay, Shel, whatever you say."

Angry, and wondering just how far her sister would go, Shelley lightly touched Brock's arm. "The grand tour seems to be over. We might find some cool at the creek." She pointed through the screening trees to where the permanent waters glinted like green glass.

"Fine," he clipped off.

Brock parked the Jeep on the high ground, beneath a stand of the drought-resistant bauhinias. They showered pink and white blossom on the hood and the bonnet.

The waterholes, billabongs, lagoon and creeks that criss-crossed the Channel Country's great cattle stations, the finest in the nation, were an enormous unexpected contrast to the glaring red of the arid plains. On their banks it was cool and green, an oasis lined by river gums white and smooth of trunk, feathery wattles and many species of flowering desert shrubs that drew on subterranean moisture.

Malkie Creek was a favourite haunt. A marvellous swimming pool in the Dry, and in the Wet a raging torrent. Now it was aglow with dozens of desert eucalyptus, with massed pale yellow flowers and silvery buds. Even the litter layer of shed bark and leaves around the trunks looked pretty, acting as valuable mulch. Higher up, wreathing the tree trunks, were the white cassias, their leaves covered with some white powdery substance that acted as protection and gave the plant an alien appearance.

At their approach large numbers of parrots flew up from an isolated pool of water, a dazzling flash of brilliant enamelled colours.

Amanda ran on ahead, playing the *femme fatale* to the hilt. She looked a very provocative figure in a tight low-necked blue T-shirt that matched her eyes, her slim tanned legs flashing from beneath short, short white shorts that showed a little too much of her pert bottom.

Amanda in an outfit like that, with her big blue eyes, blonde curls aflutter, usually stopped men in their tracks, Shelley thought, but neither Brock nor Philip appeared to be taking any notice. In fact Shelley had the dismal thought that they seemed to be exchanging a few heated words. Philip looked very agitated.

It turned out she was correct. "Your sister is the biggest troublemaker it's ever been my misfortune to know," Philip burst out the moment he reached Shelley's side. "She doesn't care what she says or when she says it. She's irritated me more times than I can remember."

"It's nothing more than showing off," Shelley soothed. "Anyway, she's my sister, Philip, and I love her."

"God knows why!" Philip huffed.

"Were you and Brock having a few words?" she asked carefully, turning so she could see Brock stroll down to the water's edge. She was struck by the fluid grace of his body in motion. One could pick him in a crowd.

"Who does he think he is, taking me to task?" Philip crossed his arms over his chest. "He shows up after all these years—just in time to get himself reinstated in Grandfather's will—then tells me to stop putting pressure on you. As if I am!"

It was an opening. She had to take it. "Actually, you are, Philip."

"The heck I am!" He looked deeply hurt and shocked. "Don't you know how much I care about you, Shelley?" He stared at her intensely. "Do you know the things I want to do for you? I've been holding back, waiting to see about Grandfather, but much as I hate to say it Amanda's right. I should ask you to marry me."

She felt like slamming her head against a tree. It was getting so bad one might have thought she had a duty to her family and to Philip to say yes. "Philip, we're friends," she said firmly. "We're certainly nothing more. This romance you've got going exists in your own mind. I've never given you the slightest encouragement for our friendship to become romantic.''

"How come your family thinks so?" His eyes locked on hers with something like triumph. "Your father and mother approve of me. You heard what Amanda said. You know perfectly well I'd marry you in a minute."

"A minute is about as long as our marriage would last. I'm not in love with you, Philip. I'm sorry. I like you, and I don't wish to hurt you."

"You could begin to love me if we had some quality time together," he persisted, believing it to be true.

"You can't take a simple no?" She saw Brock turn away from Amanda's splashing antics. He began to walk back their way.

"Never!" Philip kept his eyes on his cousin. "You're the one for me. I've known it for a very long time. But you have to cut free from your family. We can look after them, of course. I know you'd want that."

"I don't want to talk any more about this, Philip." All at once she felt like bursting into tears. It was an awful feeling to be backed into a corner.

"I love you." Philip shook his head mournfully. "We just haven't had a chance. And now Brock's back to complicate things."

"Philip, you don't even know me," she said, very quietly.

"I think I do." He squeezed her hand. "Just beware of Brock, that's all. Unlike me, he'd snatch you up and then let you drop. I can see his eyes on you, damn him!"

As Brock closed the narrow gap Philip moved off abruptly, bending to pick up a few pebbles he intended to skitter across the water.

"Everything okay?" Brock's voice was casual. His eyes were not.

"It's the darndest thing, but your coming back, or your

grandfather's dying, or both, has resulted in all Philip's ambitions coming together."

"I take it he's decided you'd make a good wife?" His handsome face was cynical.

"I don't want it to get around, but I mightn't make a good wife for anyone," she confessed wryly.

He took her hand, leading her into the shade of the acacias, a prowling anger just beneath the surface.

"Most women would consider Philip quite a catch," he observed, his eyes on the distant figure of his cousin. "What are you waiting for, Miss Logan? A man to steal your breath away?"

"The answer to that is yes."

He shocked her by kissing her neck. "A lot of passionate love affairs end badly."

"I know that." She ought to do something. What? She couldn't move away.

"But you want it, don't you? The passion?"

"How long are you going to tempt me?"

"Maybe for as long as it takes." Again the sweep of his lips across her nape.

"You have to stop that, Brock."

"Why? You don't mind."

"I do mind." She felt so languorous she didn't think she could remain standing up.

"Do you think Philip will turn and see us?" Now he brought his arm around her, high up, beneath her breasts.

"It's not Philip who's bothering me. It's you. Your arm. You know how to touch a woman."

"You're lovely." He pulled her back against his body.

"You're not. You're a devil!"

He laughed gently, dipped his raven head and nipped her ear. "Why the hell did I bring Philip? Why the hell did you bring your sister?"

"To stop you." She could feel the warmth of his hand right through her cotton shirt. Soon she'd start sizzling. "You tell me one thing, then you do the opposite."

"You shouldn't smile at me the way you do. You shouldn't make those sharp little comments. You shouldn't smell like a flower. You shouldn't have such soft, beautiful skin."

"Oh, careful, Brock!" She grabbed the arm that encircled her. "They're coming back."

"They'll take a while. Meanwhile I'm going to hold you. I can feel your heart, just under that little pink button."

"You're getting a lot of pleasure out of this, aren't you?" She scarcely knew what was happening to her the level of excitement was so high.

"Aren't you?" he murmured, for a moment believing in simple happiness. Loving a woman. Giving her as much as she took from him.

"I'm like a cat on a hot tin roof, more like it," Shelley said, the tip of her tongue curling over her upper lip, all unaware of it.

"That's interesting," he purred. "All right, Shelley, if you're in so much panic and dread Philip might see you…"

"Devil!" She glanced back at him, her head resting beneath his shoulder, saw a smile on his mouth.

"When I'm with you, Shelley, all my good intentions waver."

"Tell me the truth, Brock. What do you want of me?" She searched his eyes, part of her thinking this couldn't possibly be happening.

"What if I said everything? What would you do then?"

She felt seared by the taut leap of fire in his silver gaze. "You kissed me when I was sixteen because it thrilled you. You don't even remember."

"Oddly enough, I do. I think I must have been watching you all night. You wore a green dress."

"I did."

"It had sequins, something glittery all down the front."

The most exquisite yearning washed over her. "It was the most beautiful dress I'd ever owned. I felt quite unlike myself in it. Like a princess. You could have had any girl you wanted, but you kissed me. It was like a dream or a fairy tale.''

''I'd give anything for one of those kisses now,'' he said, putting frustration into it as they saw Philip and Amanda begin their trek back.

''Your parents haven't gone into Koomera Crossing, have they? They're at the homestead. I admire your courage and determination, Shelley, but I think you're fighting a losing battle with your Outback Adventures scheme. It has a lot going for it, but it seems to me you're desperately under-capitalized and underresourced. You must get little or no help.''

She flushed, averted her head. ''Listen, Brock, it may surprise you, but I can manage.''

''For how long?'' he countered. ''I'm with Phil on this one. You'll wear yourself out and your family will let you. Phil might think you'd make the perfect wife, but he and you would be a disaster. He'd crush all the life out of you. Him and his godawful mother.''

''Whom I suspect would rather have me murdered than allow me to marry her son. It's all madness anyway—'' She tried to turn away from his powerful magnetism but stood hypnotised.

''And I'm not in the mood for it. I just want you, alone in this quiet, peaceful place. Life is so short and full of heartbreak. You're right about revenge, Shelley. It burns in me. After my mother died I was nearly mad for a time. I hated my grandfather. I hated Frances. I hated myself. Then revenge burned past the grief. Hating people isn't pleasant. I'm not a saint, like you.''

''I'm no saint either, Brock, so get me off the pedestal.''

''Compared with me you are. I should warn you, Philip is basically weak. He always was. Frances made a mess of him. But he's going to be strong about this one thing. He thinks if he remains steadfast and patient you're going to eventually fall into his arms. Maybe with a slight push from your family you will succumb. Your sister is certainly anxious to get you out of the way."

"Amanda only wants me to marry well," she said loyally.

He couldn't suppress a cynical grunt. "Since when has your sister looked out for your interests?"

"Please, Brock, don't go on about it." She passed a hand in front of her eyes.

"I don't think you've ever been allowed to forget."

"I'm the one who survived." It took an effort to hold in the anguish. "Emotions are more powerful than reason."

"I can't argue with that!" His striking face was dark and moody. "And I'm no good for you either—I'm sure you'll agree."

"It's quite simple, Brock. You just need a woman to be kind to you," she said, before she could stop herself.

"You sweet little fool!" He caught hold of her shoulders. "I can have all the women I want."

She could taste the truth of that in her mouth. "So you have a power over women! And some power over me. I can't deny it. Men like you thrive on control and mastery, so I don't delude myself you have any special interest in me."

He relented, drawing one lean finger slowly down her cheek. "You can pretty well forget that. You yourself have power. I'm nowhere near as bitter or as angry when I'm with you. There's nothing much of you—you certainly don't flaunt yourself like your sister—but you have an appeal that she can only struggle for. I'm sure she recognizes that from time to time. It can't make things easy. After I leave here I have to go home to the viciousness of Frances and the terrible arrogance still in my grandfather's eyes."

They were very close. Face to face. "It'll be over soon, Brock," she promised him. "You'll be able to walk freely."

"Always with the memory of my mother—because she'll always be with me. As for my adventurer father! God knows whatever happened to him. Where did he go? What did he do? How can a man just go missing? A couple of years ago I ran up a lot of bills trying to trace him. No luck. It's like he vanished off the face of the earth.''

"Maybe he doesn't want to be found? Maybe he wiped the memory of his wife and child from his mind? Some people can't cope. If they stay they think they'll explode.''

"God, I've looked at it from every angle. He certainly didn't want to take responsibility for us. That broke my mother's heart. Broke her spirit. Set her up for endless humiliations. You'd have thought Kingsley was the rejected suitor rather than her father. Two men who loved her, locked in dreadful conflict.''

"You have reasons to be angry, Brock,'' she said, thinking she might be talking of herself. Fierce wretchedness was etched into his handsome face. "I get angry too. In a sense both of my parents died to me after Sean died. My father takes refuge in alcohol—oh, you'll hear about it, if you haven't already—and my mother is afraid of the world. She's retreated to her bedroom. But you have something to hold onto. Your mother believed in you. She must have thought it probable her father would try to assuage his guilt by offering you what you seem the only one competent to have—Mulgaree and all that goes with it. She must have known you would eventually have the power.''

"That's eerie,'' he said, fixing his remarkable eyes on her. "They were almost exactly her words. Why do you think I've held on? Why do you think I've come home to what is still a battlefield? This land has great meaning for me. Mulgaree is my home!'' His vibrant voice resounded.

"It's pretty awful for Philip, though. He must feel desperately inadequate. Never the grandson Rex Kingsley wanted.''

"Hell, you'd think it had worked out with me.'' Brock stared off towards the lagoon. "Philip would do a lot better in a different environment, away from such a cold and disapproving woman as his mother. As soon as I can I intend to kick Frances out.''

Never an aggressive person, Shelley shuddered. "Is Philip too to be turned away?"

"Do you want to save him as well?" He rounded on her.

"His very vulnerability commands my sympathy."

"Well, I spend little time on it." His answer held contempt. "You sweet, tender, compassionate, marvellous woman." Far from being admiring, his voice had a decidedly cutting edge.

"I won't let you make a fool of me, Brock." She looked back at him hard.

"That's what I like about you," he responded. "We could take this further, however, they're nearly here. What a shame Phil couldn't fall in love with your sister. He might take on an entirely different personality. She's so bubbly—just to cite one of her outstanding assets—while Phil always acts like he's carrying the weight of the world on his shoulders."

"Have a heart, Brock. It must be in there someplace."

He held up a staying hand. "Stop now, Shelley, or you'll have me in tears."

"Not you. You've got too much steel in you."

"How do you actually know?" he challenged her.

"I'm very perceptive," she said simply. "And why, oh, why is Mandy starting to run in this heat?"

He shrugged, turning to follow her gaze. Amanda was zig-zagging across the boulder-strewn sand. "I suppose it's because she's so playful."

"No. That's not it," Shelley said with a worried look. "Philip seems to be taking cover."

Brock's scant attention suddenly sharpened. "It's a kangaroo." His keen eyes registered movement through the trees. "It's coming after them. She's probably got a joey in the pouch."

"Oh, hell!" Anxious to protect her sister, who was given to panic, Shelley took off, far fleeter of foot than Amanda. Female kangaroos were much smaller than the adult males, but mothers of all species could be dangerous when protecting their young. This kangaroo, a red, must have sought relief from the heat, finding her way down to the cool of the creek to drink and nap.

Why was Mandy screaming? She should know better, but obviously she was frightened. Their father had always taught them not to exhibit fear with wild animals.

Brock, thinking much the same as Shelley, erupted into motion. He took off after Shelley, but the kangaroo, at once aggressive and defending its young, continued to bound after its prime target—Amanda, who was further exciting the wild animal with her shrill squeals.

Shelley reached her sister at last, heart pumping, hair streaming. She brought her crashing to the sand, urgently warning her to be quiet and lie still. It was quite possible the kangaroo would lose interest if they played dead—but Amanda seemed powerless to stop, her whole body shuddering.

Next thing Shelley knew her body was covered by a man's. Even half smothered and near crushed by his weight she knew with every fibre of her being it was Brock. Mind and body were in total agreement. His arms locked around her, forming a protective shield. They were safe. Safe. But he wasn't.

"Shut the hell up," he ordered Amanda fiercely, then took a deep breath. The agitated kangaroo, going much too fast to stop, descended on him with one bone-jarring slam, its animal scent strong, muscles spasming continuously, its fur rank and bristling.

Amanda, on the bottom of the pile, was still making frantic little cries, but though no sound escaped Shelley, pressed hard against her sister, all her muscles were locked tight, her body bathed in sweat. It was Brock who was taking the brunt. A fighting kangaroo, an adult male, could rip a man to shreds, she agonised. An agitated female, with one or more joeys in its pouch, could do a lot of damage with its powerful clawed feet.

Brock felt pain as nails racked him. Cursing to himself,

he concentrated on protecting the women. Where the hell
was Philip? The kangaroo might take off at the sound of a
vehicle or the blare of a horn. But no sound came. Instead
the kangaroo squeezed him tight with its flaying front feet
but then, finding no resistance, decided to make a break for
it. It bounded off, accelerating across the burnished plain,
leaving behind it a cloud of fallen leaves and red dust.

Brock gathered himself and stood up. The kangaroo had
slashed his right arm and, he realized as he brought his hand
around, his back. The fingers of his hand brought away
blood. He reached down, pulling Shelley to her feet.

"Okay?" Her elfin face was dewed with sweat but all
her concern was for him.

"I'm fine, thanks to you." She was dismayed by the
blood.

"I did nothing out of the ordinary. I wasn't going to have
you or Amanda harmed." He bent to retrieve Amanda, who
came up covered in debris, hot, panting and swearing her
head off.

"What were you trying to do? Squash me? Bloody hell,
just look at my knees," she moaned, as though she was a
prima ballerina about to go on stage.

"Would you rather we'd left you to get mauled?" Brock
didn't attempt to suppress his disgust.

Amanda glanced up at him, then shook her head. "Why
would a kangaroo want to pick on me? I wasn't doing a
thing. They're such birdbrains!"

"That happens with females," Brock said pointedly.
"Something in the way you were running, certainly the way
you were screaming, alarmed it. It was carrying a joey.
Maybe it had a couple more in the pouch," he explained
shortly.

This was one selfish, self-centred young woman. She
hadn't breathed a word of thanks to her sister, who had
flown to her assistance. If he hadn't been there it would
have been Shelley's tender flesh that was ripped.

"Brock, you're hurt," Shelley said, moving closer to inspect the long bleeding slash on his arm. There were more on his back, judging from the blood seeping through the rents in his shirt. "I'm so sorry this had to happen. We all know kangaroos can be aggressive, but that was a one-off. We have to get back to the homestead so I can clean that up. It must be painful?"

"It's stinging; that's about all," he said impassively. "I'm sorry I had to crush you, but there was no other way." He whirled around, his eyes narrowed. "Where the hell is Philip? Up a tree? Do you wonder why I love the guy so much?"

Philip, who had crouched down behind a boulder, rose and came towards them, looking overwhelmed by relief. "Thank God you're all right!" He made a beeline towards Shelley.

"I'm fine, too, thanks for asking," Amanda ranted, her pretty face full of outrage. "You've reached new heights today, Philip. Like the guys on the *Titanic*—you saved yourself before the women."

"What did you expect me to do?" Philip flushed. "It happened so fast. Brock was closer to you."

"Like hell he was!" Amanda, white as chalk, put out a frantic hand and pushed at Philip blindly. "You're a bloody coward, that's your trouble."

"It takes one to know one." Philip, unprepared and already off balance, staggered back.

Shelley ignored both of them. "I'm truly sorry, Brock. But we can't stand here talking. Have you had a recent tetanus shot?"

He laughed a shade discordantly. "I'm in no danger, Shelley. Don't look so worried. It looks worse than it is. And to set your mind at rest I had a shot about six or seven months ago, after I was involved in a minor incident with a guard dog I was attempting to calm."

"I feel sick," Amanda said, regarding her scraped knees as though the injuries were life threatening. "I've been coming here all my life and nothing like that has ever happened to me.''

''Then you've been lucky,'' Brock said tersely. ''When you're confronted by wild animals, and they look aggressive, you stand perfectly still. Try not to show fear and never scream. Surely you know that?''

Amanda regarded him with a mixture of habitual coquetry and contrition. She ran her hands provocatively over her body, pretending to dust herself off. ''Easier said than done, Brock. I'm not as well bush-trained as Shelley. Thanks, Shel.'' Her blue eyes went to her sister. ''I'd have done the same for you.''

Philip wasn't going to let her get away with that one. His eyes sparked with anger. ''That's good, coming from someone who's let Shelley take the blame for—''

''Please, Philip,'' Shelley cut him off. ''Let it drop. We've all had a fright.''

''Is that your explanation, Phil?'' Brock drawled. ''You got a fright?''

Philip was direct in his answer. ''I knew you could handle it. We grew up together, remember?''

''So there were no surprises,'' Brock said.

It was cool and rather dim in the homestead's first aid room, so Shelley switched on the light. Her heart was like a racing engine. Even her legs were quivering. Brock had that effect on her.

''You'd better take off your shirt,'' she said. ''It's ruined, I'm afraid.'' It was difficult to damp down her feelings in the confined space. Brock really filled a room. So high-powered it was intimidating.

''Here—don't worry about me.'' Abruptly he started to strip off the soft blue denim shirt. ''I can do it myself.''

The sexual attraction between them was sparking around the room, charging the air. He didn't know what he'd do if she laid her hands on his bare flesh.

Shelley drew back a little, biting her lip. ''As you wish.

I'll just get things ready for you." She went to the wall of cabinets, assembling a box of cotton swabs, dressings, a bottle of antiseptic, finally a basin and a couple of clean hand towels. "This should do the trick."

She turned back to face him. That was when she was beset by excitement that verged on panic. Desire. Need. To be held against him!

He had a superb body—that came as no surprise—but naked to the waist his male beauty was sublime. It left her badly shaken. His darkly tanned skin was so polished it almost looked oiled, his wide shoulders tapering to a lean, narrow waist. His body displayed strength, power and perfect proportion. She wasn't even at a safe distance. She was right in the danger zone. So close she experienced thrill after thrill, primitive and steamy.

God, help me! Heat suffused her veins and panic welled up. She was acutely aware colour had washed up into her face, betraying her. She tensed, and with a great effort freed her eyes, turning to fill the basin with warm water, then pouring in a measure of antiseptic, watching the water cloud. Everything was in slow motion, but she was so agitated she wasn't aware of it. Normally she was swift and economical in her movements, but nothing was normal around Brock Tyson. He knew perfectly well how fiercely sexual she found him.

The silence was as taut as a highwire. Shelley couldn't take her eyes off him as he swabbed the long gash on his arm. He made no sound. Didn't even give the slightest flinch, though it must have stung.

"It doesn't need stitching?"

He shook his head. "I've had worse gashes than this, and I'm a good healer. There won't even be a scar."

"That's good. Your long sleeve saved you." Though he'd worn it rolled up to the elbow. "I don't think you're going to be able to manage your back." She had to breathe very quietly, so she gave no sign of how she was feeling, but she could see the answering strain in his face.

His gaze rested on her so intently he might have been trying to mesmerize her. "So you do it."

"Okay." She recovered her nerve. Cautiously, very gently, as though this man was a panther, she began to clean the long scratches.

She could feel the excitement rising with every passing second. The urge to slip her arms around him was enormous. She wanted to press her lips to his polished skin. She wanted to let her hands travel. His broad shoulders were shielding her face and her body from him, otherwise he would have been able to read her transparent expressions in the long wall mirror facing them.

When she was almost finished he reached around and suddenly grabbed her wrist, an action so surprising she gave a little gasp. "Come here to me."

She desperately wanted to. Feared to.

Something like an electric current shot through her body, the force of it astonishing. Brock knew exactly what he was doing. He had anticipated her response exactly. Shelley Logan, innocent virgin, a girl from the bush. Never in her life had she felt such a violent reaction. She might just as well have been an unbroken filly he was winding in...winding in...through the silence bouncing off the walls.

"I could love you, Shelley," he murmured, low-voiced, folding her unresistant body into his embrace.

She shook her red-gold head, catching a glimpse of the conflict and prowling turbulence that was in him. "There would be too many consequences to falling in love with you. We're not even taking it gradually," she warned.

"Maybe it's my nature. And yours." He drew her ever closer, mindless of his lacerations, the gentleness of his movements not matched by the intensity in his eyes. Slowly, so slowly she was flooded with longing, he brought his mouth down over hers, just barely kissing her, the tip of his silken tongue sliding backwards and forwards over her lips, tracing their contours as though he found them exquisite.

It was wickedly, wickedly seductive.

Her eyes filled with tears. In truth she was dazed at the changes that had come over her, the way she could respond with a passion she hadn't even known she possessed.

"Shelley, what is it?" He drew back, his face taut.

"Haven't you got enough to worry about?" she asked, edgy with emotion.

"I forget when I'm with you." His voice was unfamiliarly tender. "I don't start out to do this. I don't determine to kiss you every time I see you. I don't want to risk hurting you. I can see you think I will."

She stared back at him. "You told me you're in a state of deep confusion about your life. Is it possible you're casting about for someone to ease the pain?"

"And I've found you? Surely you don't think this is a flirtation?" He lifted her triangular face to his, staring into the emerald eyes that glittered with tears. "I'll stay away, if you're going to find it easier. But I'll never let you marry Philip."

"How could you stop me?" she flared.

"Very easily. I'd make you pregnant so you couldn't leave me."

His words shocked her, sending a great charge through her nerves. "You're still wild, aren't you, Brock Tyson?" she accused. "You shouldn't talk to me like that."

"I shouldn't. But things happen." He gave way to his driving need, taking up the soft openness of her mouth again. "How do you know I'm not deadly serious?" he muttered as they came up for breath.

"Heartbreaker." She felt the faint delicious rasp of his beard against the soft skin of her throat.

He held her, both hands at her waist. He could easily span it she was so slender. "Or is it simply that I care about you? Green-eyed Shelley Logan with hair like flame."

"But the timing's bad?" Shelley could almost hear Brock say the words to her.

"So now you know the risk you represent."

"Especially when you're a man not noted for your restraint."

"You'll pay for that," he growled, bringing them even closer together.

"Why have you never been passionately in love, Brock?"

"It hasn't been something I'd allow." He went back to kissing her throat.

"But surely it's not a question of what one allows? Doesn't it just happen?"

"That's the problem," he said wryly. "It can happen in moments. Overnight. It can happen with the wrong person at the wrong time. Passion can destroy lives. Then again, it's a gift. Even if it doesn't last. Sex isn't passion. Passion doesn't happen as often as you might think. It takes a man and woman over, until they're knocked off their feet."

"So you know what it's like to want a woman very badly?"

His smile was a little twisted. "I've wanted many women very badly, Shelley. From time to time. Just like they've wanted me. But at heart I'm a gentleman. I won't destroy your life. I won't even take up your time if I'm going to make you uneasy or afraid."

"Afraid?"

He caught her chin. "It's written on your face."

"What else is written there?" She invited his answer.

He gave her a long, searching look. "A kind of dreaming, not untouched by anguish. You're as powerfully attracted to me as I am to you. We've found that out. But at the same time you want to run away and hide your pretty head."

"I'm a lot stronger than that, Brock."

A smile lifted the corners of his mouth. "I guess you are. Actually, I want what's good for you. Philip isn't, even if your family are pushing for it. Emotional blackmail must be one hell of a strain."

"Since my parents lost Sean—" she began.

"And you didn't?" He fixed his eyes on her.

Her face took on a faraway expression. "I lost part of myself."

"Because you're a twin. But you haven't really lost Sean because he continues through you. He's somewhere around, I bet."

She swallowed, shaken by his sensitivity, the strong current of communication between them. "He's there every morning of my life." Her mouth quivered. "I'll grow old, but he's forever a little boy. My little brother. I didn't do any wrong, Brock. I'm sure of it. Only I can't remember."

"You couldn't have done anything wrong." He spoke roughly, out of compassion, taking her by the delicate shoulders that had been forced to carry too big a burden. "You were a young child. Six, for the love of God! What about Amanda?"

"I don't know. I don't remember that day. All I can recall is high-pitched screaming. I suppose that sound will always remain with me. When I was growing up I thought my father hated me because I'd survived, but maybe he just can't stand the agony of looking into my face."

Brock knew exactly what she was talking about. Hadn't his grandfather always turned away from his light eyes? His runaway father's eyes. "That's an appalling situation, Shelley. Yet he's let you step into the role of provider?"

"Oh, no." She shook her head vehemently. "Dad's the boss. I know Wybourne is run down, and the income my scheme brings in helps, but somewhere along the line Dad lost the will to keep things going. Maybe even the will to live. He would have continued to work hard for Sean, so he could pass Wybourne on to him. That's what it was all about. Providing for Sean. Now, probably sooner rather than later, Wybourne will have to be sold."

Brock had half known that already. "So having Philip for a son-in-law would be useful in your father's eyes?"

She flushed. "You can see their reasoning. It involves security."

"But it's all wrong. I can't understand your willingness to allow your family to use you, Shelley."

"You'd accept it more readily if you could see how my parents are," she answered, stung. "You're right, of course. My parents are hiding behind closed doors. My once fine, upstanding father at this very moment is on a bender. Shocked? My mother, denied her husband's support, is locked away from the world. I simply can't bring myself to leave them."

"They might be better off," he said harshly. "At the very least you wouldn't have the life drained out of you."

"So there you are. We're both caught up in dilemmas, Brock. Both of us have walked hand and hand with tragedy."

"Are we that much alike?" It was said more in acceptance than question.

She had found him a clean white T-shirt of her father's to put on, disposing of the ruined denim shirt. She fully intended to replace it the next time she went in to Koomera Crossing and told him so, though he briskly dismissed the suggestion.

Amanda reappeared in a purple tank top over flower-sprigged cotton jeans, thinking it was maybe time for some afternoon tea.

"That's very kind of you, Amanda," Philip said, knowing perfectly well Amanda wanted extra time to fascinate his cousin. "But we must get back to Mulgaree. We can't leave Grandfather for long."

Your mother either, Brock just stopped himself from saying. Had his uncle Aaron not been tragically killed, Frances would be getting ready right now to take over as mistress of Mulgaree Station. It was all she had ever cared about anyway.

Nothing in the world created as much trouble as money, Brock thought. Money and the quest for power. It could be very destructive in families. It had ruined his.

CHAPTER SIX

THE desire to be rich in her own right had had a big bearing on Frances Kingsley's life. Born of hard-working but struggling parents, she had insisted on a good education as a means of getting ahead. Both parents, secretly in awe of their strong-willed, ambitious only child, had juggled two jobs to send her on to university—where, she had informed them, she was most likely to meet a suitable husband.

Blessed with striking good looks and a flair for dressing, she had gone single-mindedly about her studies—graduating with a degree in Economics—always on the lookout for the scion of a wealthy family. Most scions had realized her objectives very early, having been well prepared for such eventualities by their parents. Aaron Kingsley, son of multimillionaire cattle king Rex Kingsley, reared in the bush had not.

Desperately in love, Aaron Kingsley—for the one and only time in his life—had defied his father. He'd married the young woman of his choice. It had taken him less than six months to decide he'd made a huge mistake. Their marriage had been a farce.

Astonishment had faded and disillusionment set in. Under his very nose his bright, supportive, good-natured, hungry-for-sex girlfriend had turned into a different person. A person who wasn't in love with him at all—who in fact disliked having sex with him—who wasn't delighted by his little jokes, wasn't the least interested in anything that was troubling him. Like his rocky relationship with his domineering father. Who was cold.

Maybe if Aaron Kingsley, a decent young man, had married someone else he might have taken more care with his life. He might have been more ready when the rogue steer charged him.

Frances, the young widow, had made sure she'd fallen pregnant early on in the marriage to secure her position, and continued to live in a very rich man's home. The house of her father-in-law. Rex Kingsley. He'd been prepared to keep her and, far more importantly, his grandson in the style which Frances had taken to like a duck to water. Nevertheless Frances had found it difficult, given Mulgaree's isolation and Rex Kingsley's eagle eye, to meet new men. She wasn't frigid, as poor Aaron had thought. It was simply that she'd married him on a cool, professional basis. He hadn't been the lover she'd wanted.

That was how her affair with Gerald Maitland had started.

Frances greeted him at the airstrip. "Gerald, dear, how are you?"

No one would have called Gerald Maitland handsome. He had a heavy face. He had lost a good deal of his hair. He had a full mouth and thick-set jaw. He was carrying too much weight, but he was a big man and there was something important-looking about him—only natural when he was senior partner in a top law firm. He had beautiful white even teeth that enhanced his smile when he was meeting personages. The Kingsleys qualified.

"Delighted to see you again, Frances, my dear." He bent to kiss her cheek, admiring how immaculately turned out she always was. "I've missed you. How's Rex?"

"Failing fast." Frances favoured him with a smile of her own. "But his nurse is the very best. I do so rely on her. Rex is in terrible pain."

"Ah, well!" Maitland, still reasonably fit in his mid-fifties, shrugged philosophically. "I'm sorry to hear that. Money can buy most things, but immunity from death isn't one of them."

"I'm terribly worried, Gerald," Frances confided, lifting her dark eyes to him and at the same time laying a hand on his arm. "I think Rex means to change his will."

"Perhaps add a codicil?" Maitland suggested with a frown.

"No." Frances shook her head. "I think he means to pass Mulgaree to Brock."

"Surely not," Maitland protested, running a snowy white handkerchief over his bald pate. God, it was hot! "Philip has always done his duty. He's been here. He's the elder grandson, not to mention Aaron's son."

"Rex on his deathbed is seeing things differently." Frances began to steer him towards the waiting four-wheel drive. "I think he's brought you here to make a new will. To change everything. Even for me. I can't bear the thought of that."

"It mightn't happen, Frances." Maitland sought to reassure her though his own thoughts had been running parallel. He never had found out just what had happened to Catherine—beautiful, sad Catherine—and her high-spirited, high-powered son. There was a lot of animal passion in that young man. He made his cousin seem drab.

"You must let me know, Gerald," Frances was imploring him. "You're my friend. The best I have in the world. I don't think I ever knew peace or love until I met you."

Gerald Maitland, shrewd as he was, actually believed her.

Maitland had expected to see the old man soon after his arrival, but Rex Kingsley wasn't well enough to talk. He and Frances sat down to an excellent lunch served by the Kingsley housekeeper Eula, who had been with the family virtually since dinosaurs roamed the Outback.

Afterwards, to fill in the time, Frances took him off on the pretext of cooling down in the homestead's splendid swimming pool. In fact they settled for leisurely sex in the locked pool house.

Maitland, though he had loved his wife until the day she'd died, and would never have left her, hadn't been averse to taking a mistress when the opportunity presented itself. It had worked out very well for both Gerald and Frances.

*   *   *

Late afternoon in Rex Kingsley's huge bedroom, that reeked of illness, saw that stern despotic man propped up by pillows, rasping to Gerald Maitland to get down to work.

Maitland was shocked to see the great change in his client—and in so short a time. Without question Kingsley was dying. From the look of him, in a matter of hours.

"What is it you want me to do, Rex?" Gerald Maitland half turned from the small table where he had set out pen and paper, lacking a business office.

"Change my will. Why the hell else would I have you here?" Kingsley suddenly bellowed, struggling with his last spurt of red anger. "To facilitate your affair with Frances? Did you think I was such a fool I didn't know what was going on with you two? Get started, man. I have to set things right—don't I, Catherine?"

Aghast on many scores, the lawyer turned around, almost expecting to see the ghost of Kingsley's beautiful daughter in the shadows. Anything was possible in this old mausoleum.

"You can get Eula to witness it, not the bloody nurse," Kingsley barked. "Eula's a good servant. She knows her job. Of course she hates me, and loved Catherine and the boy. I could have sacked her, but I understood. Get a move on, man. You don't think it's easy for me, do you? I'm in agony."

"I'm sorry, Rex. So sorry," Maitland said, though he was filled with a terrible dislike of the man.

Kingsley's savage remark had brought home a truth. He was a fool to have allowed Frances to seduce him. That made him liable to a little blackmail. He had a fine upstanding son, who worked in the firm, and two lovely daughters, both married, giving him grandchildren. They thought the world of him. They had adored their mother.

Gerald Maitland picked up his fountain pen and sat down. "I'll take this down in longhand, Rex. When I return to the office I'll have the will properly typed up and a photocopy sent to you immediately."

"Get on with it, for God's sake!" Kingsley blasphemed, his once powerful hands clenched like talons on the coverlet.

Kingsley swiftly began to pen the most serious of words:

This is the last will and testament of Rex Burkett Kingsley, widower, landowner of Mulgaree Station, in the State of Queensland...

Eula Martin never told anyone what she knew. But she didn't think her niggling worries were a product of her imagination. She didn't like the way Frances Kingsley and the lawyer had their heads together. It was all about money, she knew. No one could amass considerable wealth without the heirs putting up a fight to get their hands on it. Miss Catherine was out of the picture. She was in her grave in Ireland. Now her son was back to assume his rightful position.

Eula couldn't remember the precise moment when it had come to her that Frances and the family solicitor had formed a closet relationship. She only knew it was years ago. Since then Frances had had no shame about inventing any number of reasons why she should take a trip to the State capital. Shopping, checks on her health, big social functions—whatever. Eula was certain Frances had managed to fit in a rendezvous with her lawyer lover on every single occasion over the past years.

Now they were talking as secretively as terrorists, at the far end of the hallway, the bright light streaming through the tall casement window illuminating their expressions. Obviously Frances was deeply upset and the lawyer was attempting to console her.

Had old Kingsley, dreadful man that he was, found the strength and natural justice to change his will? If so, Eula rejoiced. It had to be that. Of course Gerald Maitland had no right to pass on the new will's contents to Frances, but Eula was certain that was the cause of Frances Kingsley's evident distress, which looked like helpless rage.

There was not an instant to lose.

Brock and Philip wouldn't return to the house until sundown. Brock had slotted right back into station life, showing himself to be first-rate at handling the men and allocating duties around the vast station. What possible point was there in his cousin Philip objecting? Mulgaree and the Kingsley chain of cattle stations that stretched right across the giant State of Queensland was their future.

The lawyer had asked her if she could find a large manila envelope to contain the handwritten will, duly witnessed by him and herself. Eula decided on the spur of the moment she'd go a step further.

In desperate times one had to take desperate risks. Since Gerald had made her aware of the contents of Rex Kingsley's new will Frances had been literally beside herself. She could speak to no one.

Not yet.

Brock had joined them for dinner, handsome face mocking, eyes aglitter, as though he knew very soon he would be lord of all he surveyed.

"How did the day go, Gerald?"

He addressed the solicitor, but Frances intervened. "Let's hope you're not too disappointed, Brock." She gave him a bitter smile.

"Stop teasing, Frances." A warning light came into Gerald Maitland's eyes. "It's confidential, my boy. But you'll know soon enough. Poor Rex can't have too much longer to go."

"It must bother him the thought of facing up to his Maker." Brock couldn't sympathize. His grandfather had treated them all with a callous hand.

Jealousy was a very powerful force. Frances knew from her lover that Rex Kingsley had left her and her son well provided for, but were they supposed to fall to the ground and kiss it in gratitude? The real power had been passed to Brock, who possessed far more formidable natural skills than his cousin and was already demonstrating them, even in the short time he had been back on Mulgaree. Philip, her son, had been bypassed.

It wasn't to be borne. The prize had been snatched from them right at the death—unless she could make a pact with Gerald, and only then after Rex Kingsley had passed away. It was only a matter of time. Days at the most. Really, when one thought about it, it would be doing the old man a great service to help him die quickly and painlessly.

Furious as she was, Frances didn't think she could carry it off.

It was barely half past six the next morning when Shelley answered the phone. She'd been sitting alone in the kitchen, having a light breakfast and wondering how to approach her father about some refurbishments for the homestead, when the shrill sound of the phone had startled her. Her spoon clattered to the tiled floor. As she bent to retrieve it she bumped her head on the edge of the counter.

"Not a good start!" She spoke aloud, fingering the bump.

It got worse. It was Philip.

"Grandfather's dead," he announced baldly. "His nurse found him an hour ago. I had to ring, Shelley. Times like these one needs the support of one's friends. Could you do me a huge favour and come over to Mulgaree? I can collect you in the helicopter."

Shelley's first thought was that it was entirely inappropriate. Her second that she didn't want to go. She took a deep breath. "But what of the others, Philip? Brock and your mother? They won't want me there at a time like this. Your mother would see it as an unwarranted intrusion."

"Who cares how she sees it?" Philip retorted, sounding thoroughly jangled. "She only cares about herself anyway. You've no idea of all the aggravations this last hour. Brock could inherit. He's acting that way. Do you realize what a stunning blow that would be to me? It would mean so much if you lent your support. Please don't object. I'd do the same for you," he added with great intensity.

He probably would. In the end compassion won out. With one possible undesirable side effect. Her gesture of sympathy for Philip might be interpreted by Brock as a kind of betrayal.

She knew the instant before the tall, athletic figure jumped down onto the scorched grass it was Brock. No one else moved through space like he did. He dominated it with his energy and precision. As he came closer she noted the pallor beneath his dark polished skin, the diamond glitter of his eyes.

"What happened to Philip?" she asked a little nervously, aware a devil had him.

"Are you unwilling to fly with me?" he asked, as arrogant as you please.

"Don't be like that, Brock." She lifted a hand to shade her eyes. "This wasn't my idea. Philip insisted he needed a friend."

"So sweet of you!" He put a hand to his strong throat, as if he was all choked up.

"I'll tell you one thing," she said, exasperated, "he hit it right on the head when he said no one really cares about him."

"Hell, it's not as though it's hard to understand," Brock retorted. "My cousin all his life did a big fat nothing for me. But he needs all the softness he can get from you."

His anger was triggering her own, the air between them crackling with tension. "If you're so much against my coming, I won't."

"Ah, please do. We don't want Philip desperately upset," he scoffed. "Who am I to stop you?"

She looked full into his dark handsome face. "You could be a little more understanding."

"Well, I'm not a nice person." He stared back at her moodily.

"You certainly aren't on occasions," she answered crisply. "But please—don't let's fight."

"But I'm eager for more!"

His eyes dazzled her. "I'll do whatever you want." She sighed. "Philip has his mother to hold his hand."

"Except she seems to have gone to pieces." He gave a grim laugh. "That's why I'm here. For once it's Philip who's supporting Mama. Frankly, I never thought Frances capable of such feeling. She may not be weeping buckets, but she's giving a good impression of being distraught."

"Maybe you've been selling her short," Shelley suggested dryly. "It's possible she had some gentle feelings towards your grandfather."

"Never!" he mocked, bending down to press a brief hard kiss on her mouth before drawing away. "Her boyfriend's there, of course. She may be trying to impress him. Probably he was brought up to believe a daughter-in-law should grieve."

"Who's the boyfriend?" she asked, realizing her heart was pounding after that short, disturbing contact.

"You mean you really don't know?" Brock gave her a cynical glance.

"I'm not exactly in on your family secrets."

"What? With Phil's high regard for you on open display?"

She glanced away, trying to hold onto her temper. "I'd feel for you too, Brock, if you'd only let me. But you're too damned proud. So, who's the boyfriend? Should I know?"

"Phil must have been too embarrassed to tell you," he drawled. "Gerald Maitland of Maitland-Pearson, the family solicitors. They've had fun and games for years now."

"Surely not?" Shelley fought a stirring of alarm.

"You don't approve?"

"To be frank, I'm shocked."

Brock laughed briefly. "You're an innocent after all."

"And it opens a Pandora's box."

"It does indeed," Brock answered, with a hard mockery that said reams.

CHAPTER SEVEN

SHELLEY found a household far more upset than she could ever have imagined.

Frances was the biggest shock. Always supremely self-assured, to put it kindly Frances was a mess. She might have been a different person. Gerald Maitland, too, was behaving as though the death of one of his most valued clients had brought him a new experience in life. Perhaps without Rex Kingsley's patronage Maitland-Pearson would go to the wall.

When it came time for the will-reading, what occurred was a far greater shock than the actual death. Shelley sat sandwiched between Brock and Philip, wishing herself elsewhere, but strangely even Frances hadn't objected to her presence. Obviously in deference to her son, the heir.

Gerald Maitland, the very picture of a high-level solicitor, sat with fingers steepled behind his departed client's impressive antique desk. All of them stared back at him with varying expressions.

When it came, it was like a great bolt from the blue. There was no new will.

Rex Kingsley had passed away before he had had a chance to sign the document. It had been drawn up under the worst possible circumstances, given the client's precarious state of health and doubts as to his lucidity of mind; he had been on strong medication.

Maitland, to save the family further distress—and by this presumably he meant Philip and Frances—had destroyed the handwritten unexecuted document as soon as he'd heard his client had died during the night. The only valid will at his disposal—signed, properly witnessed and notarised—was the one he was now prepared to read.

It was dated a scant month after Catherine Tyson and her son had left Mulgaree Station after a terrible showdown with Rex Kingsley.

If Brock had genuinely expected his grandfather would make up to him for his repudiation of himself and his mother, all the wrongs he had done to them, he was now doomed to devastating disappointment. Nonetheless, he rallied strongly, voicing serious doubts.

"It won't wash, Gerald," he said very coldly. "And don't question my grandfather's state of mind. He'd cut back on the drugs at the very end. His nurse will verify that."

"So what are you saying, Brock?" Philip asked angrily, fixing his eyes on his cousin. "We have a will. Why don't you hear it? For all we know Grandfather didn't cut you out at all. I'm not such a bastard I'd want to see you totally ignored. You're a grandson, just like me."

"Not like you." Brock rounded on him. "I have grave doubts about what Maitland here is saying."

Gerald Maitland cheeks puffed up angrily. "No one has ever questioned my ethics. My aim is always to serve the best interests of my client. I think I can safely say my firm is very highly regarded."

"By yourselves," Brock snapped back. "What right had you to destroy that document?"

Gerald Maitland's eyes sparkled with outrage. "I judged it in the best interests of the family. I stand by my decision. I believe another solicitor would have done the same. Anyway, it's too late now."

"Why don't you read the will, Gerald?" Frances cut in, wanting desperately to put a stop to Brock. "The real will. I'm sure it's just as Rex promised."

Shelley, her nerves on edge, reached for Brock's hand, half expecting he would reject it. She could feel the waves of anger and outrage coming off him like hot spice.

"Please, Brock," she begged, very softly. "Hear what it says. Then you can decide."

He stared down at her for a moment, daunting in his anger, but after a moment resumed his seat.

Philip Goddard Kingsley was named as the main beneficiary, heir to the Kingsley fortune—which was considerable when Rex Burkett Kingsley's net estate was calculated to be about two hundred and fifty million.dollars, maybe more. There were also bequests to institutions, relatives, and staff of long standing.

Frances, who had waited patiently to hear what the old man had left her, couldn't have been more shocked. She received a fraction of what she had confidently expected and her expression was livid—though her legacy was in the very early millions. She had been well provided for in life, and Philip would have more than enough to look after his mother's future needs.

Brock was totally disowned.

"I won't accept a word of this." He addressed the lawyer directly in a deadly quiet voice that eerily had overtones of Rex Kingsley. "My grandfather brought me home to tell me something. To atone, if you like. He was leaving me Mulgaree and everything that went with it. We had words to that effect just days ago. He had come to the conclusion I was the one to run it. Philip had his chance, but he couldn't deliver. He and Frances were to be properly provided for. Was that in the unexecuted will, Gerald? Can you tell us that?"

Gerald Maitland shook his head with great regret. "I gave my reasons for destroying the document, Brock. I knew speculation would only cause pain. I swear I tried to alter things in all fairness, but the terms of the unexecuted will were not as you hoped."

"Why should I believe you?" Brock asked, not disguising his contempt.

"I'm a highly respected lawyer."

"I have no great regard for your profession," Brock said

with a hard edge. "Lawyers have lost a lot of ground. These days people don't confuse the legal system with justice like they used to. Your prestigious firm is mainly into hefty fees. There's also the fact you've managed to get away with conducting an affair with a female member of my family—may I remind you, your clients—for many years now. I wouldn't call that ethical."

Gerald Maitland threw up his hands, his florid skin blanching. Frances had convinced him no one in the family had an inkling of their affair because they'd been so discreet. So much for her smug beliefs. They weren't worth a bumper. The old man had known, and now Brock.

Philip looked at his mother strangely. "Affair? What affair?"

Shelley's body tensed. She could see in Philip's eyes that he knew nothing about it. She turned her head, conscious of Brock's scornful gaze. "Did you have to air that?"

"Their dirty little secret?" A smile twisted his mouth. "Have I hurt Philip, tender-hearted Shelley? Okay, we'll explore that at a later date. This is all too damned pat, Gerald. I won't be taking it quietly. Especially since my grandfather told me his intentions."

Gerald Maitland suddenly recovered himself, mounting a challenge. "This is all hearsay, I'm afraid, Brock."

Shelley spoke up, for the first time grateful she was there. "Brock told me he'd had a conversation with his grandfather during which Mr Kingsley assured him Mulgaree would be his."

"For God's sake, Shelley, whose side are you on?" Philip burst out in astonishment, not even trying to hide his jealousy. He caught her arm, staring into her face.

"Why don't you get your hands off her?" Brock suggested tightly.

"Perhaps someone can tell me what Shelley Logan has to do with any of this anyway?" Frances started to vent her frustrations. "These are family matters. She isn't family and never will be."

Brock laughed shortly. "Knowing you, Frances, one can see why she wouldn't want to be. I believe everything that has been said here is a lie."

"So what are you going to do?" Frances looked at him with absolute hatred not unmixed with fear. "Call the police? There's no lie. No conspiracy—"

"Did I say conspiracy?" Brock cut in bluntly. "Perhaps I should consider it."

"Now that, my boy, is a tremendous insult." Gerald Maitland's bloodless lips were pressed very tightly together. "You might apologise to your aunt."

"Not me," said Brock. "She's not my aunt either. The fact is my grandfather could well have signed a new will naming me as principal beneficiary—only that would scarcely suit, would it? The new will is now destroyed, without anyone having sighted it. Your answer is you wished to spare the family pain. Obviously you overlooked me. So could there possibly be a conspiracy to defraud the estate? Or is that inconceivable? A man like you, Gerald, wouldn't want to go to jail. But you could never count on a person like me not pressing charges. And there's Eula, the witness. I know she was called in to sign; she told me herself this morning."

"She had no knowledge whatever of the contents of the document. She merely signed." Gerald Maitland allowed his fury to show through.

"It's illegal to witness a signature without actually seeing that signature written. Sorry, Gerald, there will have to be an enquiry into this matter of the second will and why you found it so necessary to destroy it. It's possible you've got yourself into big, big trouble."

The helicopter lifted off the ground, but they didn't head towards Wybourne, as Shelley had expected. They flew into the heart of the open desert. Heartsore, she realized Brock was near to snapping point so she made no protest. She remained silent until they touched down on the flat, fiery terrain that marched on to the mirage-stalked horizon

The landscape burst into sound as a response. A great flight of white sulphur-crested corellas swirled above the mulga, while a herd of emus—some with their striped chicks—rose from behind the thick screening of saltbush to take off at a great rate, plainly outraged by the loud noise of the rotors that now gradually slowed to a stop.

"I'll take you back in a while." Brock lifted her down like a bundle of feathers. "Right now I need time to recover."

She heard the torment in his voice, understood it. It was easy to sympathize with his mood of utter disillusionment. "I'm in no hurry."

"So my grandfather continued his torture to the death?" he mused bleakly.

"That would have been too cruel. He did beg you to come home."

"You didn't know him." He took her hand. "I suppose to have found his conscience would have been too radical a change. It could be true, you know. The whole damn lot of it. To the end he devoted himself to smashing me like a pane of glass. Punishing me for not bringing my mother home."

Some instinct told Shelley that that wasn't the case. "I think that's taking your grandfather's bent towards vindictiveness too far. You said yourself he didn't want everything he'd worked for run down or broken up and sold. That could happen with Philip and Frances in charge."

"Would happen, you mean," he said bluntly. "Poor old Phil! Now he thinks it's all happening he's getting cold feet about the responsibility."

"Can you blame him? It's a big job. And he has his mother. She's no fool."

"Philip would fight her over you." His eyes flashed over her, lighting her up like electricity.

"Except there's no possibility of a Philip and me. I thought we'd agreed on that."

"Even with all that money?" He struggled to keep the bitter cynicism out of his voice, but failed.

"Don't turn on me, Brock," she begged.

"Okay, I apologise. I'm humbled by your high principles. You're the most honourable of young women. I'm blessed to know you."

"Stop it," she said, very quietly.

He emitted a deep sigh. "Do they really expect me to swallow all that?"

"Would Maitland try something criminal?" she asked doubtfully.

"He might if it were made worth his while. He could marry dear Frances, for instance."

"I can't see him going so far."

"Seeing corruption in action is always a profound shock. I don't trust either of them."

"No, but you have to remain calm so you can think clearly."

"Well, this is the perfect place to do it." His grip tightened. "Even at the worst times this country has nurtured me. When I was a boy I spent so much time in the desert. Much as I loved my mother, I hated to go home. My grandfather was so cold and cutting people were genuinely afraid of him. He had a look that could turn you to stone. And then there was Aunt Frances—and Philip, a boy like me— plotting to keep deep divisions in the family.

"Mulgaree was so fraught with intrigue we could have been back in the Middle Ages. Can you blame me if I was forever wondering about my father? Where he went? Was there nothing of a fighter in him? Couldn't he stand up to my grandfather? Hell, even I could. Yet as a small child I loved my father, and I could have sworn he loved me. I have so many questions, Shelley. Why did he put his love for my mother behind him? Is there something of him in me? Could I desert my wife and child?"

Shelley drew in her breath sharply. "I'm absolutely certain you couldn't."

"How can you be so sure?" he asked with grim humour. "You've said I have a devil in me, don't forget."

"You *are* a devil, when you want, but you're full of other things. Good things. You're even wonderful at odd, unexpected moments."

"Maybe I'm a different person with you in my life."

"Am I in your life?" She lifted her head to meet his gaze.

"For better or worse." He contemplated her gravely.

"Then let's hope it's not worse."

They walked along in near silence, looking out over the vast saltbush plains, drawing the pure, unpolluted air into their lungs. At this time of day the eroded hills, home of the yellow-footed rock wallabies, appeared purple against the piercingly blue sky.

The mirage was still abroad, as it had been from sun-up, mischievously creating chains of dazzling lakes in the arid wilderness so silvery-blue they glazed the naked eye.

Paintings and engravings were hidden away in the caves and gorges of those hills. They were reminders of the ancient tenure of the aboriginal people, for forty thousand years the most isolated of all peoples, cut off from all contact with the outside world. It was small wonder they worshipped this land.

"Where are we going, Brock?" she questioned as they moved through the spirit-driven landscape. Its extraordinary silence was almost tangible, broken only by the chatter of birds and the soughing of the acacia-scented breeze.

"Where do you want to go?" He had his thumb on the blue and white translucence of her wrist.

His sheer excitement invaded her, making her spirit open to him. She had a mad desire to say, Anywhere, with you, and barely brought it under control. "Perhaps we could go as far as the hills?"

He halted briefly, still swinging her hand. "I mean seriously—if you could go some place where would it be?"

"Would you take me?" She felt real pressure behind her ribcage. She realized now she couldn't protect herself from this man. She couldn't withdraw her heart.

"Be careful what you wish for."

"You don't think I'd be safe with you?" A poignant little smile touched her mouth.

"Not the way I am these days, Shelley girl. You offer exquisite comfort."

"You're afraid of what you might do?"

He looked down at her. "Outside of my mother, I've never had a woman tug at my heart." There was a hard ache in him that momentarily escaped.

"You don't want that?"

"Tugging on the heartstrings can hurt a lot," he said, handsome mouth down-curved. "You haven't answered my question. Where would you go? Anywhere in the world?"

"The ocean." She didn't hesitate. "The Pacific, the Indian. I don't care. I've never seen the ocean."

"God, I suppose you haven't." If anyone was trapped by love and concern for her family it was Shelley.

"There's such a lot I haven't seen and haven't done."

"That's easily fixed." A certain tenderness softened his expression.

"Money, money, money! It's hard to do anything without it."

"Probably why your family was ready to sell you off to Philip. Wait until they hear he's inherited Mulgaree. They'll be ecstatic."

"I have trouble with what we heard today."

His whole demeanour darkened. "It's Maitland's word. He heads a highly successful legal firm. Still, he's acted unethically."

"Do you mean with Philip's mother?"

He halted so abruptly she thought she might have offended him in some way.

"Of course. But you have to take my word for that. My mother and I were well aware of what was going on between Frances and Gerald. Kingsley being Kingsley most likely knew as well. Perhaps it amused him, in a devilish kind of way."

"Wouldn't Gerald Maitland hate doing something that would put his career at risk?"

They walked on, lost in speculation.

"People who know a great deal about the law know best how to break it," Brock responded grimly. "I don't believe what he did—or said he did—was open and above board. The difficulty will be to prove it. Then there's the time factor. The case could take years. Forget the scandal."

They were approaching the base of the hill country and she could see the little wallabies moving among the rich chocolate rocks streaked with yellow, magenta and blood-red. "Can you?" she asked.

He was silent for a moment. "My family is full of scandal."

"There's a lot of gossip about my family as well. Not on the level of yours, of course. The Logans are small fry. But it seems to me this whole business of the unexecuted will is on slippery ground."

"As are you." Brock caught and steadied her, one hand at her elbow as a section of rubble gave way beneath her flat-heeled shoes.

Small rocks of curious shapes that probably would have yielded all sorts of fossilized marine life, crustaceans and frogs, rained down the slopes, the sound carrying a long way in the desert. It stirred up a group of red kangaroos and yellow-feathered emus that took off for safer ground, the kangaroos bounding, great tails acting as balance, the huge flightless birds easily outpacing them.

"I suppose we shouldn't explore too deeply," Brock said, taking a quick look around. "Bound to be snakes. But they'll do their utmost to keep out of our way. Is it too hot for you?" He turned to inspect her small face. Both of them were wearing akubras to shelter their heads from the blazing sun, wide brims at a tilt.

"I'm used to it."

Masses of red-gold tendrils like licks of flame encircled her face, her skin the texture of a white camellia. It was flushed with heat and exertion, and little beads of perspiration gathered beneath her lustrous eyes and above her top lip. He found her so sexual. The ever-present desire hit him with such force it almost knocked him off balance.

He wanted this woman and the want would never go away. As he looked into her eyes he was moved to believe he not only wanted but needed her. A thousand threads seemed to bind them, growing stronger by the day.

Already caught in a maze of emotions, including betrayal, confusion, despair, and a grief that he had spent a lifetime keeping to himself, Brock realized he was within a hair's breadth of taking her.

Minutes dragged on as they stared at each other.

"Are you all right?" she asked breathlessly, painfully aware of his brooding expression and the throbbing intimacy between them.

"We should go back." He came to a hard decision. Hurting this girl would tear the heart out of him.

Something about the way he spoke, the glitter in his shining eyes, made her heart lurch. "I thought we were going to find a cave? At least we could take a look inside the largest of them. Just up there."

She pointed to a mesa-shaped dome with a single ghost gum growing at a peculiar angle guarding the cave's entrance.

"There could be some rock drawings. It might make you feel better. Just a few minutes before you go back to all your problems. Mine too."

"It could be dangerous," he warned, not talking about the terrain at all.

She gave a choked little laugh. "Did I hear right? Brock Tyson talking danger?" She grabbed his arm, using it as an

anchor to bring her further up the slope. "Come on. I dare
you."

As soon as she found firm footing she took off like a
gazelle, as though a wonderful Aladdin's cave was about to
open up for her.

"Stop, Shelley." His tone was so inherently commanding
she obeyed. "I'll go first. I'll decide whether we go in."

"Okay, boss." She tipped her brim, trying to act cheerful
when she was feeling a whole range of emotions: excitement, anguish for Brock, a kind of trepidation for herself.

Apart from the lone ghost gum, with its chalk-white bole,
there was little vegetation around the mouth of the cave
except for a broad hanging cascade of some desert plant
bearing innumerable tiny scarlet balls.

Moving carefully, Shelley picked her way to the top,
watching Brock's tall, lean figure disappear into the semi-
circular entrance. She stopped once to breathe deeply. It was
eerie.

Those little scarlet balls must be the plant's flower-heads
and they were releasing some aromatic odour like frankin-
cense. The scent grew stronger the higher she climbed. It
wasn't any kind of grevillea or hakea, or any of the widely
distributed desert plants she was familiar with and had
drawn in detail. She hadn't even seen it before, but the incense was drenching, invading her nostrils and making them
flare.

She paused at the entrance of the cave, leaning against
the striated rock wall with its furrows of multicoloured
ochres. She felt a little dizzy, as though the rich, alluring
aroma was overcoming her.

"Shelley!" Brock's tall shadow fell over her. "What's
the matter?" He came right up close to her, focusing on her
face. "Damn it, it's the heat," he rasped in a kind of self-
disgust. "We shouldn't have covered so much ground. I
blame myself and my mood. I felt like walking off the edge
of the world. Are you okay?"

He caught the point of her chin, turning her face up to

him. It was so delicate, her colouring so exquisite, she reminded him of some ethereal creature in a Old Master painting.

"I'm fine!" She tried a smile to cover up her slight feeling of disorientation. "Have you ever seen that plant over there?" She pointed to the blazing red hanging clusters.

He frowned, forcing himself to focus on the brilliant display. "I don't think I have. The perfume is very strong. Rather like incense. You'd better come inside the cave for a few minutes," he said in concern. "It's amazingly cool in there."

"Any rock paintings?" she asked, only too aware he was deeply disturbed. This complicated man.

"Wait and see."

It took a few moments for her to adjust to the dim light after the blaze of the sun.

"Well?" He watched the quick play of emotions across her expressive face.

"Oh, Brock!" The interior of the cave began to take form and Shelley looked around her in amazed delight. The space contained strange, secret things! A gallery.

They might have been inside some prehistoric temple. The dome of the cave was high, its depth shallow. The floor of the cave, perfectly flat, with a tracery of lizard imprints, was ochred sand.

She threw off her akubra, feeling the cool air on her overheated scalp. Her fingers speared into the red-gold silk of her hair, loosening it within its ponytail. Then, with something approaching wonderment, she lifted her head to study the painted ceiling.

It had to be a strange creature from another world. One skeletal white hand was lifted in a gesture that seemed to her more like a farewell than a greeting. The yellow head was as round as the sun, with red rays drawn all around it, and something like wings, but not wings, more like primitive flying devices, protruded from the shoulders. The feet were like the claws of a wedge-tailed eagle.

"A visitor from another world," Brock remarked quietly. "I just hope we haven't disturbed him."

"Oh, goodness me, no!" Shelley shivered as much from the mesmeric power of the cave drawing as the sudden drop in temperature. "It's really quite eerie. And who are all these people?"

She shifted her gaze to the scores of little stick figures who appeared to be dancing to some irresistible ceremonial music.

"I feel privileged to see this, don't you? Do you suppose he's a god? He looks like he's come from another world, like the famous Wondjina paintings in the Kimberleys. Non-human beings."

"It's hard to get interpretations," Brock said, moving closer to the rock wall to examine the little figures so simply drawn yet so brilliantly conveying movement. "That fellow up there on the ceiling looks like a sky traveller, or a mythical being who settled down in this particular cave. There must be tens of thousands of cave paintings all across the Centre and the North. Ours survive because they're right off the tourist map. Are you feeling any better?" He risked glancing over his shoulder to where she was standing.

"I'm loving this," she said. "Aren't you glad I made you come up here?"

To temptation that had never been surpassed? Brock thought.

"What a day!" he said with fierce intensity, his face all taut planes and angles.

"Yes, what a day!" she echoed, herself filled with torrents of emotion. "It all seems too much to contain. I'm so sorry, Brock, for the way you're being treated. When I think how your grandfather—"

"Deceived me?" he cut in, starting to prowl restlessly around the cave. Movements that put her irresistibly in mind of a caged big cat.

"I was going to say made you a p-promise." Her voice wavered at some expression in his eyes.

"We should go, Shelley." He was determined to resist his feelings and made severe by the effort.

"Yes, I'm sorry. You didn't want to come up here anyway."

She bent her head, a flower on a stalk, apparently not even daring to look at him for too long. The tension was tremendous. Like an actual grinding force. Everything would be all right as long as he didn't touch her.

She stooped to pick up her hat and then, straightened in one graceful motion that was unconsciously sensuous. Brock was unbearably aware he wanted her to keep going.

She was almost at the entrance when directly outside the cave a bird whistled so loudly, so shrilly, it was like an actual alarm. Already unnerved, she started violently. The involuntary cry that emitted from her throat was a shade hysterical even to her own ears.

"Oh, damn!" She knew she wasn't handling this terribly fraught situation well. She was too inexperienced. Brock had lived in her imagination for too long. She wanted him to reach out and hold her, not stare at her in that sombre fashion. How could a man with shimmering eyes look so brooding? There was strong emotion she knew he wanted to keep under control. Anything could send it crashing.

She moved urgently then, her pride coming to the rescue. Inadvertently she brushed his body as she passed. He wasn't blocking her path, but somehow she almost walked into him.

Sheer yearning! It had to be the incense from the desert plant. She was almost drunk on it, reeling slightly on her feet, her heart going madly. Her hand came up to half-cover her face.

It was then Brock lost it. With a bitter pang he realized there was no stopping him now. Her innocence and beauty disarmed him, and he was an emotional mess. He wanted her as badly as he'd ever wanted anything in his life.

He reached for her on a sharp intake of breath, with a swift movement sliding his arms down over her, pulling her to him, enfolding her slender body. It was no use trying to fight this. He had left behind reason.

His mouth closed almost brutally on hers and her lips gave way instantly under the hard consuming pressure, as though his passion for her beat down all resistance. The sheer delicacy of her tongue! She was so small when measured against him, yet she seemed to fit his body perfectly, as if she were made for his pleasure.

She was wearing a white ruffled blouse with little buttons down the front. Buttons his questing hand found, undoing them with an expertise he wasn't proud of, flipping the soft fabric back so he could take the weight of her small silky-soft breast in his hand, thumb and forefinger caressing the already erect nipple. A berry on cream.

He could feel the tremor that ran through her, hear all the fluttery sighs that rose and fell as he gave attention to her other breast, bending her backwards and lowering his head so he could take that sweet berry into his mouth, barely grazing it with his teeth.

It was better than his fantasy. A groan came from low in his throat. With every minute his desire was growing fiercer, fully-fledged.

Let her go. *Let her go.* Free her! A voice in his head made some attempt to stop him, urging restraint. Only she was clinging to him, her responses inflaming him further.

It was wonderful. It was terrible. Both in equal measure. His will was gone. The only thing that mattered was having her in his arms, his hands caressing her magical flesh, his mouth taking hers, over and over. Even in the driving heat of his passion he knew he was receiving as well as taking. They were kissing each other with such ardour and abandon anything seemed worth it.

He lifted her off the ground, pressing her body against him so she could feel his powerful arousal. Her sweetness flooded him, making him realize what his life had been like before he'd met her again. Shelley the woman—not the enchanting schoolgirl of his memory.

She was yielding her whole body to him, her face burrowed into his neck, the glorious tangle of her hair all around them.

"You should stop me." His voice was urgent as he tried desperately to collect himself, a light sweat gathering over his body.

"I can't," she whispered. "I don't want to." She couldn't get enough of what he was doing to her.

"Even when you know what's going to happen?" His hand moved to her lower back, pressing her ever closer to him.

"I told you, I don't care." She laced her arms around his neck. "What has my life amounted to up to now? Nothing. I've had no soaring joy. Don't ask me to forego it, Brock. I can't. I'm going into this with my eyes wide open."

"But you're a virgin?" he asked with intensity.

"There's no point in denying it."

"Shelley, Shelley," he moaned, "What am I going to do with you?"

"Make love to me." Her impassioned voice resonated in the cave. "Don't worry about it. You can't bring me to this pitch then stop. It's a safe time for me."

"I wish I could believe that," he said harshly.

"Look into my eyes." She held his face with both hands, staring back at him. "On my honour. I would never trap you, Brock Tyson."

"Trap me? My God!" That struck him as absurd. He could feel her whole body quivering in his arms, her naked breasts positioned against his chest like white roses. "You must tell me if I hurt you."

"You won't hurt me," she murmured, already feeling a series of piercing aches start up between her legs. They were painful and exquisite, as if minute splinters of glass were causing tiny hot slashes within her womb. It was an unnameable rapture that demanded fulfilment.

Gently, Brock urged himself, though he was feeling anything but gentle. He felt as though he had an endless capacity to ravish her. But he had to go slowly. He imposed control on himself. This would be her first time. An experience that would stay forever in her memory. It had to be blissful, not full of regret.

He laid her out on the sand, her lovely limbs extended, smoothing her clothes away from her until her naked body was fully exposed to his sight.

She was exquisite, more beautiful than he'd imagined. He bent over her reverently, placing his hands on her breasts, curved pink and white. His tongue teased the nipples while his hands moved freely along the length of her silky flesh, smoothing, caressing, down over her hips, her thighs, her waist, her taut quivering stomach, until he reached the tiny lick of flame that guarded her sex. He opened his mouth and entered her very gently with his tongue.

"Brock!" Her whole torso arched up in galvanic shock, almost lifting off the ground.

"I won't hurt you." He half lay across her, watching her face. Her expression revealed pleasure out of control, terror. For moments the two were fused as she struggled with revelation.

Never, never had anyone touched her there. Now Brock was, in the most intimate way a man could touch a woman. The excitement was so violent she felt unable to prevent herself from opening to him.

He lifted her light slender legs, as weak as a kitten's, and slid them over his shoulders, pausing for a moment to gauge her reaction. Her responses were more important to him than his own ever-intensifying hunger.

Now her eyes were tightly shut, but he murmured to her as he explored her body, whispering beautiful endearments like a ritual for her alone.

She felt him rise above her to take her mouth deeply. Felt his dark shadow. The scent of herself was on his tongue. Her small breasts thrust against his hands. There was so much heat inside her. It was like being slowly consumed.

He drew out the stimulation, teasing, taunting, adoring,

himself lost in erotic pleasure, until she was losing all breath, her head lolling back, her arms and legs spread wide. It was then he slid down over her, his body slick with sweat, no longer able to contain himself or the urgent passion he felt for her.

This was the moment. Their moment. His shaft was rock-hard and then he was inside her, on his way to ecstasy. A starburst of pleasure he had never experienced before.

CHAPTER EIGHT

As HER senses began to return Shelley opened her eyes to Brock's face. He was leaning over her as she lay naked on the sand. She was sighing voluptuously without knowing it, filled with the strange feeling that her body wasn't her own any more but his.

"Shelley!" He stroked the wild tangle of damp curls away from her face. "Are you all right? I was a little worried."

She didn't answer, but continued to stare into his eyes, jewels in a dark copper mask. Her initiation into the rites of love seemed to be the only real thing that had happened to her in her entire life. Even the terrible trauma associated with the drowning of her beloved twin was steeped in mystery, almost like a ghost story.

"You wanted me as much as I wanted you." He spoke with tenderness. This from a man who had so recently shown the full range of wild passion.

"I think you must love me a little," she said dazedly, huge eyes lustrous, her breath still unsteady.

She was trying to take in all that had happened. The tiny aches and hurts in her body told her it was no fantasy. They really were one flesh. She knew this man, body and soul, but never in her most erotic dream could she have conjured up such an extraordinary sexual encounter. A great storm of emotion when her every want her every need had been fulfilled. How long had it lasted? She didn't know. She might even have lost consciousness so great was the stimulus.

He remained above her, gazing into her eyes. "Perhaps I do." His answer was barely audible as he bent to kiss her.

"How do you feel? I tried hard to be gentle but I must have hurt you."

"At the beginning," she answered gently. "But then I was—possessed. I wanted everything you did to me. You're the most wonderful lover. You've taught me what making love is all about."

He stroked her cheek. "Lovemaking only becomes special when a man and a woman truly care about each other. Then it's a communion of bodies and a communion of souls."

"Yes," she agreed dreamily. "I didn't know it was possible to feel like this. The downside is, I don't think I can get up. I don't think I want to. I want to stay here in this cave with you for ever. I'll always think of it as our cave." Tears filled her eyes.

"Please don't cry, Shelley," he begged, his tongue gathering up a single tear, only to swallow it.

"Don't you know women cry when they're happy?"

"That's all right, then." He slowly leaned forward to kiss her waiting mouth, his lean body superbly naked, totally unselfconscious with it. "I want you again," he confessed. "You've seduced me."

"I want to." Delicately she let her hand move down over his velvety body, feeling it tremble beneath her touch.

"So what are we going to do about it?" he demanded, his voice deep and husky. "I was supposed to be taking you home. I should be back on Mulgaree, mourning my grandfather, guarding my own interests."

"Instead you're with me," she whispered, lifting her arms to link them like the lightest chain around his neck. "I think we've earned ourselves a little piece of heaven after what we've both endured."

"To have you like this always," he muttered, sliding an arm beneath her beautiful naked body so perfectly constructed for his loving, entering her again powerfully.

The entire family in its wisdom was waiting for her when she arrived back on Wybourne. It was sundown and the sky was a glory of deep crimson and gold, with long streaks of pink, yellow and amethyst on the horizon. It was a spectacular change after the blazing blue of the day.

"Where have you been?" Amanda demanded to know before Shelley even put a foot on the verandah where they were now assembled. "You left Mulgaree hours ago. Where have you been?" she repeated, frowning blackly.

"With Brock, obviously," Shelley said, trying desperately to act normally, convinced she couldn't possibly after her life-changing experience. When she wanted her family they were never there. When she didn't want them she had their undivided attention. "That was him flying the helicopter. He's pretty upset. What business is it of yours anyway, Amanda?" Shelley did a rare thing. She rounded on her sister.

"Come into the house, Shelley." Her father rose from his planter's chair, giving the stern order. Once a handsome man, with good features and black Irish colouring, Patrick Logan looked what he was: a sick wreck, his looks and health eroded by drink and grief. But at least he was sober. Her mother, too, was present, hovering like a blonde shadow of herself near her father's shoulder. In their youth and up until the death of their little son, the Logans had been a popular, fine-looking couple, hard-working, with every expectation of a good life in front of them. The tragedy had affected both parents profoundly. Both had cracked wide open.

"You've got sand all over you," Amanda accused, her eyes moving all over her sister, cold with suspicion. "You haven't been up to any tricks with Brock Tyson, I hope? He has that reputation."

Shelley flushed violently. "That would be the first thing you'd think of, wouldn't it, Mandy? You've got such a lily-white reputation yourself."

"That will do, Shelley," her father suddenly roared. There was no way Shelley was allowed to attack her older sister. "Amanda is right to ask. We were worried about you. Philip Kingsley has rung several times."

"What on earth for?" Shelley felt a great spurt of anger. Who the hell did Philip think he was? Her husband?

"He wanted to know why you weren't home," her father replied, as though that were reason enough. "You left Mulgaree shortly after two p.m. We all had fears you might have crashed."

"More likely Philip had fears I was with Brock," Shelley answered sharply, forgetting to keep her tone respectful. Her father had a hair-trigger temper, though he had never struck her. He knew she wouldn't have tolerated that. Maybe he knew as well. "Philip is very jealous of Brock. I'm sorry if you were all worried. Brock wanted a little time out. He landed in the desert. He's always loved it there. It gives him comfort."

"So that's where you got the sand?" Amanda continued to stare at her sister, picking up immediately the fact that there was a change in her. Shelley, after an afternoon in the heat of the desert, looked ravishingly pretty. And ravished? Amanda glared at her.

"I'd really like to take a quick shower. May I? It was so hot."

"Make it very quick, Shelley." Her mother spoke for the first time. "We have things to discuss."

When she returned, in fresh clothes and smelling of boronia, her family was sitting in the living room, her father staring at his knees, her mother with her eyes shut, Amanda almost on fire with impatience.

"Sit down, Shelley," her father said, lowering his gaze from her face the way he always did. "I took the first call from Philip. He confided in me about his grandfather's will. As I understand it he is the main beneficiary—Rex Kingsley's heir. Mulgaree is his. The other boy, Brock, was not mentioned in the will. Personally I find that totally un-just, though I suppose it's none of my business. He was a hard, hard man, Kingsley. Cruel, really. I can't imagine why he brought the boy home."

"Brock's not a boy, Dad. You remember the boy. He's very much a man. Philip couldn't hold a candle to him."

"So much for that!" Amanda, her father's favourite, hooted. "It's Phil who's got the money. He must be worth millions and millions. Oh, God, I wish he was attracted to me, but it has to be you."

"You're welcome to him," Shelley said.

Her father glanced up quickly, a strange light in his faded blue eyes. "I hope we can all come together on this, Shelley. Philip tells me he loves you and he's ready to marry you. Isn't that enough for any girl? By the way, I should tell you I cancelled that party of tourists who were coming out here. I don't like strangers around the place. I know they've brought in money, but we won't need it now."

Shelley felt it like a betrayal. "Oh, Dad, why did you do that? I have everything planned. They'll feel very let down. I'll have to give the deposits back. You should have consulted me. We do need the money."

Her mother leaned closer, took hold of Shelley's hand. "Listen to your father, Shelley. Don't think we don't appreciate how hard you've worked on your project. We do. You're a very clever, capable girl. You could be anything you want to be, given the opportunity. Now you have it. No young woman in her right mind would turn down Philip Kingsley. He can give you the world. Moreover, he's prepared to do it."

Shelley felt her face burning. "Except I don't love him, Mum. When are you going to take that into account? I'll never love him. He doesn't attract me in that way."

"Not like Brock, I suppose?" Amanda broke in, expression taunting. "I agree he's very sexy, but he's not the type to offer marriage."

"We're not talking sex here, Amanda." Patrick Logan stared at Amanda angrily. "But we are talking marriage. That's a most serious business. The most important in a woman's life. Philip is a good-looking, decent young man. All right, he never was a patch on his cousin, but he's young and healthy and love will come later. You both have many interests in common, Shelley. You'll be a great asset to him.''

"Dad you're not listening," Shelley cried out despairingly. "I'm not interested in Philip."

"Then you'd better get interested in him," Patrick shot back. "He'll devote his entire life to looking after you. He loves you, you fool of a girl. You should be honoured."

"And think how he can help us," Amanda piped up in all seriousness. "If you became Mrs Kingsley that would be a big step up for us. The Kingsleys are important people. Now his grandfather has gone Philip will be rich and powerful. He'll probably blossom and gain in confidence. If you gave him a little help he could turn into the man you want him to be."

Shelley stared incredulously at her sister. "What are we talking here, Mandy? Prostitution?"

Patrick Logan's face turned beetroot with anger. "You should go and wash your mouth out with soap. I won't have you speaking like that, Shelley. What we're talking about is making a good marriage for you. We love you."

"Do you, Dad?" Finally she decided to ask it—what she had always wondered in her mind. Shelley looked at her parents sadly. "You can hardly look at me, Dad, and Mum scurries away every time I try to talk to her. You don't love me. You bitterly resent me for surviving when Sean didn't."

"Stop now, Shelley," her father thundered, as though she had no right to broach the subject.

"Please, Dad, allow me to speak. All this avoidance of anything connected to Sean has been bad for all of us. He was my twin. My other half. He's never left me. He's still around. He wakes me every morning of my life. I talk to him. I tell him things that I can't possibly tell anyone else."

"Are you going to stop?" her father gritted, shaking his head like an enraged animal.

"Yes, stop, Shelley!" Her mother and Amanda cried together.

"Oh, yes, you'd all like me to. It suits you. Since that day you've treated me like I was involved in foul play. I was six. I can't remember much except the screaming. Everything else has gone white. I know I didn't cause Sean any harm. I couldn't have. I loved him. He loved me. He loved me more than any of you. He always ran to me. Never Mandy."

"Such a pity, then, that you pushed him," Amanda said bitterly. "Oh, don't look like you're going to faint. Everyone knows."

"How cruel you are, Amanda." Their mother spoke in shock and pain. "I never knew."

"You're all cruel." Shelley's voice broke. "One day I'm going to remember. Some little chink of light is going to fall into my brain. You've always been the accuser, Amanda, but you couldn't have been fully engaged looking after us."

"I want this to stop," Patrick Logan bellowed, actually capturing his younger daughter's gaze. "No purpose can be served by trying to unravel the events of that terrible day. Sean was loved by us all. He was my son. I don't suppose you women know what that means to a man—having a son."

"You've never given your daughters a chance, Dad," Shelley said. "Especially me."

"It's not like you're saying," her father claimed. "Are we to be condemned because you remind us so terribly of Sean? Our little Sean! He was so very, very special."

"I'm special too, Dad, if you could only see it."

"Shelley, you mean so much to us," her mother broke in, blue eyes full of remorse. More and more frequently these days she was coming to see the great wrong the family had done her younger daughter. "You're a dear girl. A strong girl. Your father and I know how difficult it's been for you."

"And me!" Amanda insisted, looking outraged.

"You look like Mum," Shelley said by way of explanation. "Sean and I took after Nana. We inherited her colouring. If my colouring wasn't so different—if I'd been blonde and blue-eyed like Amanda—you might have been able to love me, too."

Her mother hung her head in shame and sorrow, as though her deepest secret was out. "All I can say is your father and I do love you, even if we've found it very hard to put it into words. We want the best for you. And the best for a woman is a good marriage. You can work wonders on Philip if you try. He's a one-woman man. He'll be faithful to you."

"We just want you to have security," her father urged, as though that was the greatest goal in life. "Philip is coming over in the morning to formally ask my permission."

Shelley was thunderstruck. "You've got to be joking, Dad. Ask your permission? Am I wrong? Are we not in the twenty-first century? Is Queen Victoria still on the throne?"

Patrick Logan looked as if he was running out of his scant store of patience. "It's the right and proper thing to do," he said, looking as if he believed it. "I am your father. Lots of people do it. It may be old-fashioned but I consider it a necessary courtesy."

"I think it's kinda cute." Amanda touched her father's hand, backing him. "Think it over, Shelley. You're on a winner here. And if you're on a winner so are we."

Shelley made sure she was the first to greet Philip—though greet was hardly the word. More like confront. Philip had a blind spot. Her parents were about to sell her off to the highest bidder. Her sister, only four years older than herself, was fully in agreement.

They made it sound as if all their thoughts were of her and her future. Her security, her position in life. When in fact the whole lot of them were thinking of the benefits to themselves. Her marrying Philip was obviously intended to help them out. The Logan family fortune, such as it was, had dwindled to an all-time low, despite Shelley's best efforts, and it was her job now to restore it by making a good marriage. This so-called marriage of convenience. God knows, it still went on. Love alone apparently wasn't enough for some people. A strenuous attempt was being made to hassle even harass her into it. Well, she wasn't falling for that one.

And what of Brock? What would Brock think when he found out Philip had come over to see her?

Her mother had been giving her worried looks all morning, otherwise she might have thought her mother was secretly thrilled. It broke her heart that such a thing as a marriage between herself and Philip Kingsley could inspire such rare pleasurable emotions in her mother. She even looked younger, brighter. She was wearing one of Amanda's summery shifts and she had shampooed her hair, fluffing it up into soft curls. It was easy to see how pretty she had been and could be again. Even her father wore a smart casual shirt and trousers instead of his usual dingy T-shirt and shorts.

It was as though what they so ardently wanted just had to happen. Fate owed them. They needed a helping hand up.

But Shelley was filled with a wild rebellion. I'm no sacrificial lamb, she fumed. Even if I married Philip I'd have to slit my own throat. Let Amanda find herself a millionaire to save the family fortunes.

She stood well back until the rotors of the helicopter had stopped, watching Philip jump to the ground, looking immensely spry. Her father was right. He was good-looking when he wasn't looking defeated. This morning he looked triumphant, like a man coming to claim his bride. She inhaled deeply, then let it out. She reminded herself to keep calm, nevertheless there was only so much she was prepared to take.

"Shelley!" he called to her in delight. "I didn't expect you to come down for me. I was going to walk up to the homestead."

"We can drive," she said, waiting for him to reach her. "But first we're going to have a little talk. What do you think you're doing here, Philip? You can't be serious about asking Dad for my hand?"

His expression underwent a rapid change. "But, Shelley, I thought you'd be thrilled."

"How did you come to entertain such a wild idea? I've told you in every way I know how that I have no romantic interest in you. We're friends. Period. Where do you get off, spying on me? Ringing the house yesterday? Three or four times, wasn't it?"

"I was concerned about you," Philip protested. "I don't trust Brock. Not with any woman, let alone you. I love you deeply. If you let it love for me will come."

"Oh, rubbish!" she said angrily, not caring now how much she hurt him. "I—do—not—love—you. I know you're finding that very hard to deal with but it's true. We have a friendship of sorts. If you persist, we won't even have that. How dare you presume to think you could speak to my father about marriage plans? My plans don't include you."

"Because you're stubborn, Shelley," he insisted. "You like to fight things. You would love me if you gave me a chance. I explained that to your father. Your parents like me. They approve of me. Isn't that important to you? Don't you want to help them? A marriage between us could bring them back to life. I'm a very rich man. Hasn't it sunk in yet?"

"You need to consider what Brock is going to do," she said sharply.

"There's nothing he can do. The will is airtight. Would you come back to Mulgaree with me afterwards?"

"In a word—no!" she said shortly, exasperated with Philip's persistence.

"It's my mother, isn't it? She's never made you welcome. I'll change all that. Don't let her worry you. She's had too big a hold on me for too long. My mother can go. Maybe not at once, but when we're settled. She's assured me Brock's filthy claim she had an affair with Gerald Maitland is totally untrue.''

"That's the ostrich in you talking, Philip," Shelley said wearily. "You're forever hiding your head in the sand. My parents are expecting you for morning tea, heaven help them. They're as single-minded as you, but it won't make any difference. Maybe the two of us could put our great brains together on this one," she remarked flippantly. "I happen to know Amanda has need of a rich husband.''

He laughed briefly, his expression a perfect copy of his snobbish mother's. "I have no interest in Amanda whatsoever. In fact I can't believe you're sisters. I find her vulgar.''

"That's interesting. I'd take her before I'd take your mother. We might as well go up to the house and get this over with. But I warn you. Don't attempt to speak any nonsense to my father, or I might go ape.'' Shelley walked away quickly to the Jeep. "Did you tell Brock where you were going?'' she asked when they were underway.

"As a matter of fact I did. He laughed in that devilish way he has. He thinks I'm a perfect fool, but I know I'm not. With Maitland there I might as well make my own will and you can witness it. I have huge responsibilities now. I might even be able to work out a plan to help Brock. I'm going to have need of him to ensure our operations run smoothly. He's a pretty cluey guy and he's tough. The men respect him. What do you think?'' Philip turned slightly to stare at her. "He could take up Strathdownie. Manage things from there. That's bound to please him.''

"Oh, yes, I'm sure!'' Shelley said with extreme irony— only Philip missed it, gratified by her response.

"I wouldn't want you to think I didn't have a heart.''

She was terribly distressed and embarrassed by her family's behaviour. They piled on the pressure, treating Philip like visiting royalty. Philip, being Philip, lapped it up. He really was incredibly pretentious. It seemed he believed his ambition of marrying her could be achieved as soon as possible now that they'd all decided. Except for the prospective bride, who might not have been there for all the notice they took of her.

I could be a prize cow, Shelley thought angrily. Why don't I try mooing? She wondered when they would start haggling over her selling price. I'm not a human being at all. I have no mind of my own. It wouldn't even matter if I disappeared under the table or got up and screamed blue murder. All that was needed was for Philip to propose. Her family was giving him every possible indication that he would be welcomed with open arms. They didn't care a whit about her. She was the means to an end. She could see by the look on Philip's face he knew what was expected of him. There was a price to be paid but he was willing to pay it. He was, after all, master of Mulgaree—the flagship of the Kingsley chain.

She knew then that her position at home was untenable. Unless she did what they all wanted and agreed to marrying Philip her life would be made a misery. The truth was it had been a misery for years. Misplaced love and loyalty had bound her to her family. Now their total disregard for her wishes had set her free.

She had no real place on Wybourne. It wasn't hers and it never would be. It was her father's. She couldn't stop him from closing down her operation. He'd already done one dreadful thing by cancelling a booking out of hand. The agency had been very disappointed in her when she'd spoken to them and she didn't blame them.

Finally anger overcame her embarrassment. She desperately needed to get away. To be on her own to think. She would spend a few days in the town. The pub would put her up. But would her father let her take the truck? For all the hard work she'd done and the money she'd brought in, she didn't own a damned thing. She'd have to think of something. Be inventive! She could say she had to approach the general store to see if they'd take some of their supplies back. Her father would go along with that.

In one way or another Rex Kingsley's death had forced decisions on them all. Her father had made his, and once his mind was made up there was no power on earth that would shift it.

She just couldn't stay.

Shelley didn't even remember making the long, hot trip into Koomera Crossing. Her mind was preoccupied with all the remarkable events of the past few days. Her father had made little fuss when she had asked for the four-wheel drive. She'd kept to the excuse that she was returning a lot of the supplies for refund, plus she had to pick up a few odds and ends for herself. She'd told them she might stay a day or two. She had a lot of things to think over.

Her father had nodded at that, as though he knew that given time and the proper reflection she would come to the right decision about Philip's offer of marriage. After all, she owed him. She had lived when Sean hadn't.

Afterwards she had gone to her room and packed a small suitcase, carrying it out through the rear door to the large shed where the station vehicles were garaged.

No one had waved her off.

She arrived in the town mid-afternoon, exhausted, eyes sore from the glare even with good sunglasses, her back, neck and legs aching. She parked the vehicle at the back of the pub, checking in a few minutes later.

"Would you like the same room, luv?" The publican, Mick Donovan, asked her.

"Fine, Mick. I'm used to it." She smiled and waved as she made her ascent up the curving wooden staircase.

An hour later she was back on the main street after a quick word with Annie Hope, the woman running the general store. Mercifully Annie agreed to take back all the non-perishable supplies she'd ordered in.

The talk in the town was all of Rex Kingsley's death, fol-

lowing so closely as it had on that of Ruth McQueen, the
late matriarch of the McQueen dynasty, a woman as ruthless
in her fashion as ever Rex Kingsley had been. Two peas in
a pod. Two products of an era. No one in Koomera Crossing
as yet knew which way the will went—evidently Shelley
wasn't expected to know—but the betting was that justice
would be done to Brock. The whole town was behind him.

Leaving the general store, she heard footsteps rushing up
to her, then felt a hand on her shoulder. "Shelley, the very
person I need to see!"

Shelley turned, her face wreathed in smiles. She'd recognise that voice anywhere, the honeyed American accent
that overlaid native Australian.

"Christine, how lovely! Hi, how are you?"

An extraordinarily stunning, tall young woman stood before her, the picture of happiness and glowing health, un-
believably chic in long tight-legged jeans, a low-slung tur-
quoise studded belt, blue tank top, midnight-blue akubra and
high boots. Christine Claydon, ex-international fashion
model, now wife to Mitch Claydon of Marjimba Station.

"I'm fine. Never better." Christine rolled her beautiful
sapphire-blue eyes. "I've got some wonderful news for you.
I can't wait to tell you. Could we grab a cup of coffee?"

"Great!" Shelley felt a rush of pleasure. She would have
loved to have had a sister like Christine, someone so warm,
so friendly, so supportive. "I could feel the good vibes coming off you. You look gorgeous. Married life is agreeing
with you."

"I'm so happy," Christine said in a near reverential tone.
"True love is a miracle, Shelley. I'm going to pray you'll
find it."

"Maybe I already have."

"Are you serious?" Christine grasped Shelley's arm,
looking into her face very searchingly.

"I'm serious." Shelley smiled, albeit wryly.

"Oh, honey, you've got to tell me more." An expression
of great interest passed across Christine's beautiful face.

A few minutes later they were seated at a window table in the town coffee shop, a couple of cappuccinos and a plate of delectable little pastries before them.

"Your news first," Shelley prompted, settling her shoulder bag on the floor close to her.

"It has to be—it's so extraordinary! You'll never believe it." Christine broke into a little excited laugh. "We found the treasure. Claydon's Treasure."

Shelley blinked, feeling a shower of sparks. "You've got to be kidding me!"

"This very morning." Christine began to tuck in to a tiny caramel tart. "I called Wybourne straight away and Amanda told me you'd gone into town. I'm so damned excited and thrilled and it's all because of you. Mitch persuaded Kyall it was worth a shot to have another look for it. Both of them have been stuck with so much work they couldn't do a thing about it before this, but they decided to follow your hunch."

"And it worked out?" Pleasant little shocks were coming in billows. "This is amazing. And all because I thought a line representing a billabong was in the shape of a turtle. It only occurred to me because I draw. The actual map-drawing was very elementary."

Christine nodded, her eyes flashing a brilliant blue. "Turtle Creek. That's where the Claydon Treasure was buried. Right under the family's nose, so to speak. Of course they took advantage of a metal detector, which was an enormous help, but even then they had to sweep both lines of the creek. About two hours on they began to get hits, then they decided to go to work with the shovels. And bingo! The digging revealed an old, very rusty metal box."

"And what was in it? Was it worthwhile?" Shelley felt her friend's buzz right down to her toes.

"Gold is gold, honey," Christine said in a bright, teasing voice. "Gold and jewels. Mitch said it was quite an extraordinary feeling. He and Kyall started to whoop and jump around like a couple of kids. I can't tell you what a kick we all got out of it. Sarah and Kyall, Mitch and I. Not to mention his parents. The great mystery has been solved and all because of you.''

"This is really, really exciting," Shelley said, colour flaring in her cheeks. "I'm so pleased for you all. The story of the legendary cache was right after all."

"And we're so grateful to you!" Christine leaned over to squeeze Shelley's hand. "But that's not the end of it. We're all determined you're to have your reward. A nice little nest egg like you thoroughly deserve. Everyone wants to speak to you, but as the first one to see you I've got in first."

For a moment Shelley could scarcely control her breathing. "Christine—" embarrassed, she began to play with her spoon "—that's very kind, but you don't owe me any reward."

"Hey, kiddo, you're going to get it. Fair's fair. Mitch is going to confirm it. The treasure would never have been discovered without you and it's very valuable."

"All I did was point out something to Mitch. You're my friends."

"And we love you," replied Christine, clearly meaning it. "We owe you as well. I'll let Mitch explain it. We want you to visit Marjimba soon. Stay a few days. Mitch will collect you. You only have to say when it suits."

"I'd love to come, Christine," Shelley exclaimed. "In fact I'm really touched. I can't believe I've run into you today of all days. I badly need someone to talk to. Someone I trust."

"Then fire away." Concern clouded Christine's face. "Is it about your family situation?"

Shelley swallowed. "You know Rex Kingsley died?"

"Sure. It's all around the town. Say, Brock doesn't come into this, does he?" Christine made a shrewd guess. "I heard he's back. He always was quite a guy!"

Shelley felt herself flush.

"So, Shelley, what's been going on?" Christine asked, fixing the younger woman with a kindly, experienced eye.

Shelley told her.

"Surely Rex Kingsley didn't tell Brock one thing then do another?" Christine said finally. "That's particularly cruel, even for him." She gazed out of the window, thinking hard. "Brock has a strong case if he goes to litigation. It seems harsh to say this, but I can't see Philip cutting it as a cattle baron. And that's awful, your family putting pressure on you to marry him. Can't Philip take no for an answer?"

"Wishing makes it true." Shelley shrugged.

"What about Brock?"

Shelley let out a long sigh. "I couldn't help falling in love with him, Chris."

"If he's the guy I remember..." Christine grinned. "You've got it bad, haven't you?"

"Maybe I'm being incredibly naïve?" Shelley looked over at her friend. "Maybe I'm setting myself up for a lot of pain? Brock's told me he has to put his life in order. That he can't make plans."

"You don't think he's using you? Brock was a regular ladykiller, as I recall."

Shelley shook her head. "No, I don't think that. Brock is tough, but he doesn't have a callous hand. He's actually very sensitive. I think he's a little in love with me as well, but I don't want him to feel trapped. He's very bitter and angry about his grandfather and the way he and his mother were treated."

"He has every right to be," Christine said flatly. "Rex Kingsley was a tyrant. Not that my family missed out on tyrants. My own grandmother tried to control everyone and run their lives, remember? Too much money and too much power can be a very bad thing. Gran and old Kingsley were two of a kind, yet they loathed each other They must have recognised their own worst traits in each other! Brock had a very bad time growing up. It must have left a lot of scars."

"It has." Shelley answered, sadness in her voice.

Christine put out a hand to cover Shelley's with her own.

"But you're a girl with the healing touch. I think of you that way. You're brave and resourceful, not to mention lovely and capable. What more could the man want? Is he coming back to stay?"

Shelley shrugged. "Who knows. I don't think I could bear it if he went away. I imagine it all depends on the final outcome of this will."

"Would you go away with him if he asked you?" Christine gave her friend a gentle look.

"To the ends of the earth," Shelley said simply. "There is nothing for me on Wybourne. The only way I can redeem myself with my parents is to marry Philip Kingsley and I can't do that. Even if there were no Brock, I couldn't do it."

"So what are you going to do?" Christine stared at her. "You can always come to us while you think things through. It must be awful at home."

"It's not the best place to be."

"Well, my offer stands. As I said, Mitch is insistent that you visit. You can come with me now if you like. We really care about you, Shelley," Christine said with affection. "And there's tons of room."

Shelley bit her lip. "I really appreciate the offer, Christine. Let me think about it."

"Sure." Christine smiled with compassion and understanding. "You've put up with a lot. Who knows? It might work out with Brock."

"Reckon I'm woman enough for him?" Although Shelley laughed there was naked vulnerability in her eyes.

"I'd say you're just the sort of woman he's been searching for," Christine said supportively. "So act totally cool."

"Not easy when one's in love and uncertain of the outcome."

"You think I don't know that?" Christine smiled wryly. "All I can tell you is if you truly love him go after your dream."

"Even when circumstances are loaded against me?"

"Am I correct in believing you're a fighter, Shelley?" Christine looked encouragingly into the younger woman's lustrous green eyes.

"I hope so."

Christine smiled. "Then that's part of the job. Convincing Brock he needs you."

"Eula's in town," Mick Donovan informed her when she came down the next morning for breakfast. "Thought you might want to know, seeing you're friendly. You might be able to get a word out of her. I can't. She's very close-lipped about her employers is Eula. But she ordered up big at the store. Annie told me not a minute ago. It's hard to believe the larder is empty. Either that or they're going to give a big party now the old boy's gone."

"Maybe the wake?" Shelley suggested.

It was mid-morning before she actually saw Eula Martin, Mulgaree's housekeeper, grey head burrowed down, coming out of Imprint, the small, well-patronised store that sold materials and patterns.

"Eula!" she called, and watched the woman look up, her kind, jovial face breaking into a wide grin.

"Shelley, love. Don't you get around, now?"

"You don't exactly stay put yourself." Shelley went to her quickly, taking over some of the housekeeper's large number of parcels.

"Mrs Kingsley sent me in just when I was keeping an eye on things," Eula confided, lowering her voice. "Seems to me she doesn't want me around the place."

"So who dropped you?" Shelley asked.

"One of the men. It's a hell of a trip. I tell you, Shelley, I just can't understand Mr Kingsley doing what he done. Even given he was a wicked old devil, God rest his soul. Her ladyship couldn't wait to rid herself of me presence. I don't like the chances of holding onto me job now she's in charge."

"Let's go and have a cup of tea," Shelley suggested.

"Exactly what I wanted m'self," Eula said, then dropped her bombshell. "I shoulda told Brock before this, but I took a copy of that will."

Shelley stopped dead in her tracks. "Wh-a-a-t?" She caught Eula's arm. "Which one?"

"'Struth, love!" Eula looked at her in astonishment. "The one I signed only the other day. I expected Mr Kingsley to change everything but the cruel old tyrant didn't. Don't like his chances of gettin' through the Pearly Gates."

Shelley scarcely heard her. "Did I understand you to say, Eula, you took a copy of the will you witnessed?"

Although Eula's plump cheeks reddened, her voice was unashamed. "I don't feel guilty and I don't feel I done nothing wrong. Mr Maitland asked me to find a manila envelope for the will—scrawled it, if you ask me, terrible handwriting—and took off down the hallway to speak to her ladyship, who seemed real upset. Hello, I said to m'self. Something's come as a shock. I acted fast. I've got ESP, I reckon. I took off for the study and ran a copy of the will on the fax machine."

"And you weren't caught?" Shelley stared at her, her mind a riot of jumbled hopes.

"No." Eula shook her soft grey head. "They were too busy talking. Thick as thieves, those two. Don't like 'em. He's a real fox behind those white teeth. And she's plain awful. They weren't worried about me. I'm a good cook and a good housekeeper, otherwise I'm a halfwit—in case you haven't discovered yet."

"Listen, Eula, you're as sharp as a tack."

"No, I'm not, love. I have to remind m'self of things all the time. I'm goin' to have a long talk to Dr Sarah about it. You know what they call it?"

"It won't hurt to talk to Sarah," Shelley said, "but I'm sure there's nothing wrong with you, Eula. It's common to become forgetful as we get older."

"Older? You cute little thing. How old are you now?

Twenty-one? What is it they call that memory disease again?''

"Do you mean Alzheimer's Disease, Eula?" Shelley asked in concern. "From what I know of you, you're in the clear. People do gradually lose the excellent memory they had in their youth, but it's not abnormal. Just part of age-ing."

"I hope so, love. I don't want to finish up senile."

"Did you read the will, Eula?" Shelley asked, starting to move towards the same café she and Christine had visited the day before.

"Dear girl, would I do such a thing?" Eula made a busi-ness of rolling her eyes.

"Did you?" Shelley knew better.

"Never had enough time, love," Eula confessed. "Plus the fact I didn't have m'glasses. I'm blind as a bat without 'em."

"Did Mr Kingsley sign the will in your presence?"

"'Course he did," Eula said grimly, looking Shelley right in the eye. "Wasn't he supposed to? I couldn't witness nu-thin'. I'm not a rocket scientist but I'm fairly bright."

For a few stunned moments Shelley was silenced. "And where's the copy now? Surely you've read it in the mean-time? What does it say about Philip inheriting the lot? About Brock missing out?"

"When he was countin' on being reinstated? Wouldn't you? I'm gonna tell you something, love, and I don't want you to tell anyone else. Not for the minute. It'll come to me. I don't know where I hid it. See—that's what I'm talkin' about. I'm always doin' this to m'self. I hide things I don't want found and then I can't remember where I put 'em. I still can't find the only good thing I own. Ma's gold brooch. It's got little diamonds on it. It'll turn up, I suppose. It's in the house somewhere."

"But the house is huge, Eula." Shelley felt dismay. "There must be a trillion places to hide things. Was it the study? Did you shove it into a book?"

"Gracious, no. That's too close for comfort. It could be discovered. Don't worry, love. It'll come to me. Always does, eventually." Eula looked troubled. "I tried to retrace me footsteps but I was dodging those two. Thought I shoved it in a Chinese vase but I didn't. That shook me. Sometimes I can remember things I did fifty years ago better than what happened the other day."

"Don't put pressure on yourself," Shelley advised. "Keep calm, go about your business, and it will slip into your mind." God, I hope so, Shelley thought. "It's gone nowhere, as you say. It's in the house. So is your mother's brooch. Let's have that tea—and would you like something else? My shout. Now, it's absolutely vital you talk to Brock...."

CHAPTER NINE

PHILIP came home from Wybourne looking more relaxed and confident than Brock had ever seen him, even though arrangements were underway for their grandfather's funeral. Mercifully it wasn't going to be a huge ritual, like that of the McQueen matriarch. That event had involved the entire town of Koomera Crossing, with mourners coming from all over the vast far-flung South West. Rex Kingsley's funeral service was to be short and sweet. Just family. Employees apparently didn't count. That meant no tear-stained faces. No flowers. No eulogies. No mourners to read poems or sing songs the great man had loved.

Rex Kingsley was to be put to rest in the quite ghastly mausoleum he had erected for his son Aaron, Philip's father, despite Rex's stated wishes to be buried in Mulgaree's private cemetery, over a mile from the main compound and not within its grounds.

Aaron Kingsley's grandiose tomb, to Brock's mind, resembled something out of a vampire movie.

It was Philip, his grandfather's heir, who had decreed father should lie with son. And that was that. No one had been anywhere near the mausoleum since Aaron had been laid to rest there. Frances, Aaron's widow, never visited. Neither did Philip and, having made his grand gesture, neither had Rex Kingsley.

The whole depressing area, unnaturally cold within its dense grove of trees, though well maintained was off limits for everybody except the groundsmen who had the misfortune to work there. Station staff avoided it like the plague, especially the aboriginal stockmen, who claimed they heard voices coming from within.

"So what are you smirking about?" Brock asked, very much on edge.

"I think I can persuade Shelley to marry me, given a little time," Philip told him with a ring of triumph. "I have her parents on-side. Amanda is pretty happy about it as well, the mercenary little bitch."

Brock's expression turned steely. "You're dreaming."

"Dreams do come true. Shelley will come around," Philip said with surprising confidence, already a different man now he was out from beneath his grandfather's shadow. "She's no fool. She knows I have much to offer her. This is a turning point in both our lives. Besides, she's more than half in love with me already."

Brock stared hard at his cousin. "Believe that and you'll believe anything. I'm starting to feel sorry for you, Phil. This big love affair is in your own mind."

"How would you know?" Philip countered with some aggression. "You've been gone for years while Shelley and I have grown close."

"Her family have been piling more and more pressure on her to do so. Don't you find that disgusting?"

Philip smiled as though it were funny. "I do, actually, but if it helps me I don't care. I want Shelley more than I've ever wanted anything in my life."

"Wouldn't your mother be terribly angry?" Brock mocked.

"Oh, for Pity's sake!" Philip raised his head to glare. "Mother won't have a say. I'm thinking of asking Shelley to attend Grandfather's service. It's early days, but she should stand by me."

With great difficulty Brock held down his temper. "You know, Phil, there's something odd about you. You're delusional. You have difficulty living with reality. You've got everything mapped out in your head. You're going to marry Shelley Logan, bring her to Mulgaree. There's only one hitch. Shelley's not going to do it. She doesn't love you, fella. Face it!"

"She will." Philip gave him a defiant smile. "She's a stubborn little thing—that's the red hair—she likes to keep a man guessing. But I know in my heart she really cares about me."

"I can't imagine why."

"She's admitted it," Philip insisted. "I know this is hard for you, Brock, seeing me get everything I want. But I want to help you."

"How, exactly?" Brock's voice was toneless.

"We-e-ll," Philip considered. "I'm not suggesting a partnership, but I can use you, Brock. You have skills I don't. Once Grandfather is laid to rest we can get down to discussion and reach some agreement. You've been treated unfairly. It will be in my power to make it up to you."

Lightning flashed in Brock's silver eyes. "You don't really think I'm accepting this will?"

Philip smiled. "Not even you, Brock, would relish going to court over it. Grandfather was gravely ill. He certainly wasn't senile, but he was heavily drugged most of the time. It takes big money to hire lawyers, Brock. You don't have that kind of money. Besides, even you couldn't want all the family skeletons dragged out of the cupboard. Our family business made public. That would be dreadful. With time and good intentions there's a way out of this. You'd be doing us all a big favour if you'd accept Grandfather's wishes with good grace."

"Sorry, Phil. No can do. And I'm not in need of your advice. Grandfather told me very plainly I was to take over the reins. He wasn't happy with you, for obvious reasons. You're not cut out for it, Phil. I'm not so much concerned with having his wishes carried out as getting my due. And, while we're on the subject, tell me—why pick on that awful mausoleum for his final resting place? Our grandfather specifically stated the private cemetery. You're not obeying his wishes. Surely that's your duty?"

Philip's expression was open and sincere. "I've thought

and thought about it, Brock. I'm sorry you don't like the idea, but it's where he should be. With his son—my father.''

"Not with his wife?'' Brock countered. "Our grandmother? She's in the cemetery.''

"While Aunt Catherine lies buried in Ireland.'' Bitterness mixed with shame got the better of Philip. "Grandfather never forgave you for that.''

Brock's heartbeat stumbled. It was probably true. "He told you, did he?''

"Why not? We spoke a lot about it,'' Philip lied. "The mausoleum is where Grandfather belongs. A family like ours needs a centre.''

"What rubbish!'' Brock shuddered visibly. He threw up his hands in disgust. "A family like ours needs light and fresh air let in.''

"Exactly!'' Philip exclaimed in triumph. "That's why I'm marrying Shelley Logan.''

Brock finally found Shelley at Harriet Crompton's restaurant. It was closed until that evening, but through the window he could see Shelley and Harriet seated at a table, poring over a portfolio of what appeared to be Shelley's drawings.

At his first tap both women looked up, faces signalling surprise and pleasure. Harriet came to unlock the door.

"What brings you to town, Brock?'' she asked, taking in his mood at a glance. His startling eyes were lustrous but she could see a storm was brewing. When he spoke, however, his voice gave nothing away.

"Better here than Mulgaree, Harriet.'' He bent to kiss her cheek, a gesture that seemed as natural to him as breathing. Brock Tyson had quite a way with all women. "I wanted to have a word with Shelley.''

Shelley too saw the disturbance in him. "Is everything all right, Brock?'' Shelley asked, her thankfulness at seeing him turning rapidly to anxiety.

"Perfect as soon as I can find a decent place to live,'' he

drawled. "Are they your drawings, Shel? I'd love to see them."

"Look at them now," Harriet invited. "Shelley is a very talented young woman. She was better than me even as a child, when I was supposed to be teaching her."

Brock pulled a chair from another table, sat down. All of the drawings were on the large sheets of white paper commonly used in transparent technique, and Shelley had brushed washes of colour onto the pen drawings.

He turned over the sheets in silence, thinking he had stepped into a desert garden after rain. He knew all these wildflowers. He knew the glorious birds. The birds were static but somehow she had given them life. He could see their brilliant wheeling, almost feel the wind beneath their wings. Others were poised on branches. Even the branches, the odd leaf or blossom used as a counterpoint, were extraordinarily lifelike. As for the flowers! They were absolutely precious. These weren't just pretty drawings but realistic, drawn with botanical precision. Delicate calabras from the ipomoea family, the exquisite cleomes, wild hibiscus, fan flowers, poppies, paper daisies—the water lilies were superb. He could almost smell their fragrance.

"I'd really like time to study these." He stared at her. She was hypnotic. "They're marvellous. You're not only an artist, but a naturalist. They would look splendid framed, maybe a green frame, touch of gold. There's a whole collection of John Gould's Australian birds at Mulgaree. He visited somewhere around 1840, I think. Someone in the family bought them. Have you ever seen them?"

She shook her Titian head, unable to mask her pleasure at his reaction. "No, but I'd love to. Gould produced books on birds from all over the world."

"You mean to say Philip, who seems to think you're about to marry him, hasn't ever shown you?" he asked caustically. "That's quite extraordinary, given your talent and interest in such things."

"Philip, who is *not* about to marry me, Brock, isn't terribly interested in my lifelong hobby. As far as he's concerned they're just pretty drawings—the sort of thing women like to do.''

''Then we can consider him a philistine. She's very good,'' Brock said, speaking directly to Harriet as if Shelley weren't there. ''Look at the wonderful detailing on this bellflower. What are we going to do about it?''

''A showing would do nicely,'' Harriet said, greatly approving of his interest and enthusiasm ''That's the first step.''

Shelley surprised them both by saying, ''Who knows where I'll be?''

''What is that supposed to mean?'' Brock shifted abruptly in his chair. He was still uneasy after his conversation with his cousin. Certainly Shelley had exhibited quite a sympathy for Philip. Was it possible she could be talked into marriage? Could she be forced, if only by the strength of her love and loyalty for her family? Very strange things happened in life.

''It doesn't matter at the moment,'' Shelley said dismissively. ''But it seems like a miracle you've come looking for me, Brock. I was desperate to get in contact with you. I rang Mulgaree, but as bad luck would have it I got Philip's mother. She said you weren't there and hung up.''

''Charming!'' Harriet commented. ''Why don't you two go off and have a cup of coffee? I'd make it for you, but I have lots of things to do for tonight and I can see you both want to be private.''

Brock stood up abruptly, tall, lean, wonderfully compelling, his hands jammed in the pockets of his jeans. ''Thanks, Harriet. Any chance of finding a quiet table for me tonight? I'm staying in town.''

''So is Shelley, as it happens!'' Harriet announced artlessly. ''Table for two?'' Harriet closed her hand around Shelley's portfolio as though she wouldn't let it get away from her.

"All right, Brock?" Shelley looked up at him as if for permission, aware he was full of tensions.

"Of course it's all right," he clipped off. "Seven-thirty?"

"Leave it to me."

They headed out together. The main street was alive with people, the air a buzz of sound. It was Wednesday, market day, and the street stalls selling all sorts of produce, fruit, flowers, plants, vegetables, preserves and all manner of arts and crafts, were set up on the pavements, flowing onto the main street itself, which had been blocked off to traffic.

"Let's grab a sandwich or something and go for a drive," Brock said restlessly. "Obviously we've got a fair bit to talk about. What would you like?"

"Anything. Ham, chicken—I don't mind. How did you get here?"

"I drove like hell." He brushed hair like black satin in the sun off his forehead. "I wasn't about to beg for the chopper. Phil has grown inches since we all heard the good news. He's assumed the role of Master of Mulgaree."

"Well, I've got news for you," Shelley burst out, staring up at him excitedly.

He scarcely heard her. His arm shot out just in time to encircle her and draw her back to safety from a kid on a bike with no business on the pavement.

"Is it good?" His gaze slashed over her, questioning what she was saying.

"It's not about me and Philip, if that's what you mean. Why are you reacting so angrily?"

"Because the bloody fool is very serious about you."

"How could you possibly believe for a minute I might feel like that too?" Her own temper caught fire while, perversely, her great passion for him grew.

"Hey, don't let's have an argument on the pavement. Wait here and I'll go and get something for us to eat. We can fight like cat and dog after that."

*   *   *

It took twenty minutes of driving to find a cool secluded spot next to a lagoon that had been reduced by the heat and the drought to a string of pools surrounded by wide sand and clay beaches. In the Wet the lagoon was home to thousands of nomadic water birds, but now the waters lay still, the central pool deep and dark green in the middle, fed by a subterranean spring. There were tracks of emus and kangaroos on the sand, as well as the webbed feet of birds, but they were off taking a snooze in the heat. On the opposite bank was a high rockface worn smooth by the waterfalls that cascaded down it with the rains. It was dry now, and striated with ochres.

Both of them were quiet, trying to keep their raging emotions bottled up. But confusions allied to sexual energy were humming all around them.

Brock stopped the dusty vehicle beneath the welcome shade of a magnificent gum, opening his door and taking a long swig of his drink. "I've got a rug. We can set up over there." He indicated a cool shady spot stretching back from the sand to the trees.

"Fine."

"So tell me," he said, when they were seated on the rug, the neatly packed sandwiches opened up.

"You're never going to believe this—"

"Shelley," he said, taking a ham sandwich and biting into it with his white teeth, "at this stage I'm prepared to believe anything."

"Eula is in town."

"Great. Tell me something I don't know." He let his eyes move over her, caught up in a maze of emotions, amazed at their power. She beguiled him, bewitched him. He wanted to pull her down and make love to her. Over and over again. No way was Philip going to have her.

"Why are you looking at me like that?" she asked edgily. It was as if they were circling one another.

"I've had a kind of—distressing morning," he confessed

dryly. "I had to listen to Phil's deluded ramblings, for a start."

"I hope it wasn't all about me. I'm sick to death of Philip and his delusions. He's taking his grandfather's death as a signal to do what he likes. I know you're upset, but take it easy. You have to listen to this. Eula and I had a long conversation."

"Now, that's truly life-changing. Why would I possibly be interested in Eula at this point?"

"All right, if you're not going to listen—" Shelley came to her feet fast, excited and exasperated, feeling her cheeks so hot she wanted to splash them with pool water. But Brock caught her bare ankle, resting his fingers around it, sliding them seductively up her slender leg.

"Sorry, sweetheart." He stared up at her, his voice suddenly conciliatory but still with that familiar mocking touch. "Please sit down again. I really ought to curb my tongue. Eula is in town...?" he prompted.

Shelley sighed, thinking his merest touch gave her the shivers. Gracefully she eased herself down onto the rug again, her yellow cotton voile skirt that matched her sleeveless top floaty around her.

"Eula took a copy of the second will," she said, her eyes registering her hopes. "Gerald Maitland asked her to find a manila folder, and that's when she decided off her own bat she'd go a step further. While he and Philip's mother were off in a huddle Eula rushed to the study and took a copy on the fax machine."

"What an absolutely splendid idea." Brock raised his arms to the heavens. "The only trouble is, the bloody thing wasn't signed."

"Don't you believe it," she said sharply. "Eula swears it was. She's no fool. She said she witnessed your grandfather's signature."

That got his total attention. Brock stared back, abandoning his mocking attitude.

"Why hasn't this come to light? Why hasn't Eula spoken

up? Has she read it? Where the hell is it?'' His black brows
drew together, somehow recalling his grandfather.

Shelley didn't reply immediately. She tucked a long lock
of her hair behind her ear. "She hasn't read it, Brock. She
didn't have time. She hid it for safekeeping. The only
thing—''

"Don't tell me," he groaned. "She doesn't know where."

"It's somewhere in the house, Brock." Shelley suddenly
realized he knew a lot more about Eula than she did.

"Dearest girl," he said, almost kindly, "that would be
like looking for a needle in a haystack. Always assuming
the needle has anything at all new to tell us."

"I'm betting it has a lot to tell us," Shelley said.

"If we can only discover where she buried it." Brock
joined his hands. "Let us pray." He intoned. Then, in an
entirely different razor-sharp voice, "Shelley, what do you
suppose it means?"

"It means your grandfather's high-minded solicitor was
lying," she said vigorously. "Surely that's a grave mistake
for a lawyer? Though I suspect they do it all the time.
Philip's mother, if she's his lover—''

"She is," he said in an unforgiving voice.

"—is in on it. They're both guilty of God knows how
many serious charges.''

"People are likely to do anything when there's a great
deal of money involved," he observed grimly.

"I don't think Philip was in on any plan."

"There you go again! Defending the bastard."

"Any minute now I might have to tell you to go wash
your mouth out with soap. Believe it or not, that's what my
father said to me only yesterday." The memory stung her.

"Shelley, you'll have to find the strength to get shot of
your family.''

"What about yours?" she retaliated. "They're worse than
mine.''

"Agreed. Is there any possibility at all they could force

you to marry Philip?'' he asked with his brooding silver stare. "Play on your loyalty?''

"None whatsoever. I think I might take a trip to clear my head. And I could be coming into some money. Remember the legend of the Claydon Treasure?''

He raised his brows. "Who doesn't? Don't tell me you've found it,'' he scoffed.

"Mitch and Kyall McQueen found it,'' she told him severely. "Christine told me. She and Mitch are married now.''

"Yes, I know. They were always meant for each other. But what does this have to do with you?'' he questioned.

"I was the one who gave them the vital clue. I interpreted what I saw on the old map. One of those extraordinary things I do,'' she half joked. "I told Mitch the outline of a billabong reminded me of a turtle. And that's where it was—buried in Turtle Creek. It's gold, Brock Tyson. Gold. And I'm to have a reward. My friends insist.''

He was still for a moment, staring at her. "You are a one to pull out miracles. That's quite a story. I know my grandfather believed in the Claydon Treasure. He would have had a few hiding places of his own in his time. So this reenforces our faith in the old legends.''

"Yes, it does.''

"What do you suppose the reward is?'' he drawled.

"Whatever it is I'll be happy with it. It's just so exciting.''

She slid down on her back, staring up at the blue chinks of the sky through the canopy of trees. Even under the gums the heat was dense. She lifted her hands to her dewed temples. "I'd love to go for a swim.'' Heat was thrumming through her blood, her feelings for him so overwhelming they were a kind of terror.

Brock! Unforgettable Brock.

He levered himself over her, taking hold of her wrists. "Why don't we?''

"No swimsuits." Sexual tension was in the air between them. Like a blue mist that might explosively self-ignite.

He laughed deep in his throat. "There's not a soul around, Shelley. No one within miles. I've seen your beautiful luminous body, and you've seen mine. I haven't been able to get the image of you out of my mind. Look at that shimmering water," he urged persuasively. "It's so inviting. I always used to go skinny-dipping as a kid. We can leave our clothes on the rocks on the other side and swim together. I don't believe in allowing these magical moments to go by. Let's go." He saw her hesitation, the soft fluctuating colour in her cheeks.

"Oh, Brock!"

"Why so shy?" He stroked her heated face.

"Because I am." She felt bedevilled, excited, acutely aware he knew her body intimately.

"Okay—I like it." He smiled, but there was something very demanding in his expression. "Let's." He pulled her effortlessly to her feet.

"What happens if someone comes?"

He grasped her slender hips, pulling her close. "We'll dive under the water until they go away."

"All right. Give me a minute." She inhaled sharply.

"Sure." He gave her a long, appraising look that set her blood on fire.

Shelley felt herself falling...falling...falling in love. In some ways it was like a freefall through space.

CHAPTER TEN

BROCK went first, wading through the shallows until he reached the other side.

"Come on!"

Shelley was still standing where he'd left her, beneath the trees, an ethereal figure in her filmy, floaty, pale yellow dress. Maybe if he rubbed his eyes she would disappear. Then he'd be alone again. Alone for the rest of his life. It didn't seem at all remarkable that he had fallen deeply in love with her. Maybe that was the whole story of love. Instant recognition. For him, Shelley was that one young woman who separated herself from all the rest.

She was moving quickly now, running across the sand, her sandals off, splashing across the clear water, careless of her long skirt, which would soon dry off in the heat. He took time removing his own clothes so he could watch her. The little sleeveless top came off first, then her skirt, the hem sodden. She didn't look at him. Not once. But he knew inside she was ablaze. Next off came her bra and tiny briefs.

She made his senses reel. He might have been looking at an enchanting pastoral painting come to life. She looked both fragile and luscious, like a peach, her red-gold hair tousled and wild, tumbling down her back. The sun caught that tiny lick of russet-blonde at her flower. He vividly remembered his mouth there. She reached up to place her skirt in the sun, then threw up her head and made a rush for the water.

"We're both crazy!" she called, the shining light all around her like an aura.

He was crazy all right, he thought tautly. Crazy for Shelley. It took him seconds to cross to where Shelley was,

sunlight glistening off his skin, sculpting the taut muscles
of his chest, shoulders and buttocks.

Seeing him coming, so magnificently male, so powerful,
Shelley felt an enormous pressure behind her ribcage. She
could worship this man. The thought had her diving under
the water in an effort to cool off, only surfacing as he came
alongside.

"Got you!" He drew her to him, feeling the thrilling
impact of her body, water-slippery against the length of his.
He let his hands stroke all her curves. "How do you feel?"
His eyes read her. "Am I giving you a hard time?"

"Yes!" she whispered, keeping her eyes on his face. The
black lashes that so marvellously fringed his brilliant eyes
were flecked with beads of water. She pulled his head down
and slid her tongue over his lower lip, not surprised when
he responded masterfully, lifting her higher and kissing her
passionately.

She could feel the excitement rising in her like a wild
scream. They went under, still kissing, the electricity their
bodies generated spitting little gold sparks. Neither was able
to resist the other, caught in the fierce grip of physical desire.

It was so new to her. So new and rapturous. Yet with an
edge of danger. She had never felt more herself and at the
same time not herself at all. His. They swam a little, sending
up cascades of water with their hands, always coming back
to hold each other tight, their mouths fused in long intoxi-
cating kisses, entwined in sensuality, sinking under the
weight of it.

Finally the foreplay reached a pinnacle of urgency.

"I need you now." His glance was intense, a silver flame.

She was ready for him, muscles clenching and unclench-
ing deep within her body, preparing herself to receive him.

In the shallows he lifted her high in his arms. She was
so petite, so perfect to make love to. He felt humbled by
the shining trust in her eyes.

The sun moved over them, naked in their garden of Eden,

the hot golden light and the dry wind already beginning to dry their hair and their skin.

There was no drawing back. They went straight for it, the need so strong they were prepared to forget everything.

Afterwards, satiated by their lovemaking that had entered the realm of real turbulence, Shelley drifted off to an exhausted sleep, secure in her lover's arms. It was quietude after such heart-stopping ecstasy, when she'd been a slave to her senses. Now, in the aftermath, she was held gently, her hair stroked. Within moments she was lost in her dreamscape...

Her surroundings were recognisable. She was six again, in Wybourne's home gardens, though they looked more like a jungle, with water reeds and grasses so tall and thick in some places that they obscured the glassy pond like a green veil. She was holding Sean's hand, trying to console him. He was saying he felt sick. They were trailing well behind Amanda, trying to keep up, and Amanda was cross about something. She didn't want to mind them. She never did.

Shelley knew this was an unreal world. She knew something unthinkable was about to happen. Sean was crying in earnest, so she stopped and put her arms around him, hugging him, trying her hardest to soothe him. Her mother always said she was the stronger twin, being the first to make her appearance into the world.

Usually her efforts worked, but not now. It was so hot! Even with big floppy hats clamped to their heads, the sun was burning a hole in their scalps. Amanda was walking much too fast, increasing the distance between herself and them. They weren't toddlers any more, but didn't Amanda understand she wasn't to let them out of her sight?

"Not for a minute now, Amanda," her mother had said, beaming at her precious twins.

"Yes, yes, Mum!" Amanda was always so impatient. She said her mother could only ever think of the twins. Never her.

"Amanda, stop!" Shelley shrieked. "Sean feels sick.

Please, Amanda. Amanda!'' Her cries were growing frantic.
Sean was sobbing now and his cheeks were very red, burning to her touch. She expected Amanda to stop and turn
around, only Amanda kept on walking however much she
called.

Sean, profoundly upset, broke away from her, saying over
and over, ''I want to go home.'' She told him to sit down
in the grass and stay where he was. She was a good runner.
She'd catch up with Amanda and make her come back.

''I don't like, Mandy,'' Sean hiccoughed, his sweet little
face strangely sweating. ''I only love you, Shel.'' He allowed her to settle him on the grass in a shady patch, turning
up his cheek when she bent to kiss it.

''You watch how fast I run!'' She tried a silly half-start,
almost a dance. She hoped he would laugh but he didn't.
He looked as if he was coming down with one of his little
ailments.

Why was Mandy so cruel?

''Go home,'' Sean muttered. ''Want to go home.''

''We will; I promise. Hang on.''

Almost halfway, something made her stop. Fear. Confusion. A terrible foreboding.

When she turned around Sean had vanished.

Her scream almost tore the heart out of him. It was filled
with so much grief, piteous and full of horror.

''Shelley!'' He wrapped her close but she struggled and
struggled. She wasn't even herself when her eyes opened.

''It was only a dream. You're safe. Your cry almost
stopped my heart.'' He brushed the wild tangle of curls out
of her eyes.

She tried to gather herself but her heart was pounding so
much it hurt her.

''Give yourself a minute.'' She was obviously deeply distressed.

''Sean,'' she managed after a while. ''I was dreaming
about Sean.''

He turned her into his arms, subject to his own excruciating dreams.

"I've never been able to remember that day clearly." She clung to his shoulder. "Only Mum screaming. It's all been shrouded in mystery. Amanda said I pushed him—"

He was furious at this. He held it down, though his jaw clenched. "Your sister is one cruel bitch. I'd stake my life you did nothing of the kind."

"I didn't. I remember now. Sean was feeling sick. Amanda had walked away from us. She was a long way off. She didn't want to be bothered with her little brother and sister. I told Sean to sit down on the grass and wait while I ran to get her. He wanted to go home. I should have taken him then, but Mum said we had to stay with Amanda. She didn't stay with us. I ran, but when I turned around my twin had disappeared. I never thought of the water. Sean didn't like the water. He never went near it. I could swim. He couldn't. But it was so hot."

As she spoke she began to cry, tears pouring down her face.

"Let it out," he bade her, holding her tight.

"Sean died," she said in a voice so poignant his eyes stung. "It wasn't an accident. Between us, Mandy and me, we let Sean drown."

"Never, Shelley," he said, his gaze deep in hers. "God just called him home."

Eula insisted on returning with Brock in the four-wheel drive rather than wait for Philip to fly the chopper in to collect her. Though Brock tried to talk Eula out of it—he considered the trip too long and tiring for her—she was adamant she'd rather travel with him any day.

At the pub, the three of them had gone over and over the events of Rex Kingsley's last day on earth. But Eula, distress showing in her eyes, simply could not recall where she had hidden the handwritten will.

"I could have sworn it was in that big Chinese vase, but it wasn't."

"Maybe someone discovered it?" Shelley decided dismally. "If it was Philip's mother, she'd destroy it."

"Mr Kingsley signed it," Eula insisted doggedly. "I mightn't have known what was in it, but I know that much. If Maitland said he didn't he's a liar. 'Course, it's my word against his—and who'd believe silly old me before him, the big-shot lawyer?"

What they all needed was a miracle.

At Mulgaree homestead Brock found the household in an uproar because nobody could find the great key that locked the heavy double doors of the mausoleum. The interment was the following morning. An Anglican bishop was flying in to conduct the service.

"Shoot the bloody lock," Brock advised, feeling dreadful about the whole business.

"We might have to," Philip agreed helplessly. "I wonder what happened to the key? It was big enough not to get lost. Did I dream it or was it always in the top right-hand drawer of Grandfather's desk? I haven't seen it for years. Eula might know."

Eula didn't; she was too busy cursing herself for not being able to remember. Why was she so certain the will was in the big Chinese vase? The vase alone was worth thousands and thousands.

"You saw Shelley in town. Is she all right?" Philip tried to get his cousin's attention, but Brock looked grim and unapproachable.

"Why wouldn't she be all right?" Brock countered.

"Something funny is going on," Philip confided. "I rang the house and spoke to Amanda. Lord, I don't like her. What's Shelley doing staying in town?"

"Maybe she's had a gutful of her family," Brock said bluntly.

"I want her at the service."

"I don't. Leave her alone."

"You're grumpy, aren't you?" Philip said.

"Grumpy? What the hell are you talking about?"

"I'm referring to your mood. You are such a moody person."

"You don't think I have cause?" Brock looked at his cousin with open contempt and disbelief. "God, you're an idiot."

"There's no need to swear."

"Oh, for God's sake, Philip, shut up. If we can't find the key we'll have to shoot the lock."

In the end Brock had to do it, Philip was too concerned with thoughts of desecration. Both young men were in a kind of anguish, with the pall of death hanging over them, the massive disruption caused by argument over the authenticity of the will and the enduring misfortunes of the house of Kingsley.

Having opened the great door, Brock stood well back, as if he couldn't bear to go in. "I'll wait here."

"Come in with me, please." Philip, too, had slewed to a halt. "This is one hell of a scary place."

"It was your idea." Brock shrugged ironically. "You can still call it off. You know perfectly well what our grandfather's wishes were. I expect he hid the key. He didn't want anyone to come here."

"No one would have. Only he died."

It was so dark inside they really needed a torch. Aaron Kingsley's ornate raised tomb, white marble, like the floor, lay in the centre of the crypt, under the bulb-dome. The whiteness of the marble was lending some illumination.

"I suppose we should say a prayer," Philip said, his voice echoing hollowly.

"You say it. It won't help your father now."

"This place worries me," Philip moaned. "It smells like it's been closed up for a thousand years. Do you suppose it was guilt that made Grandfather build it? He never treated my father well—or any of us, for that matter." He looked towards his cousin, but Brock wasn't answering. Why wasn't he?

Brock, who had characteristically moved ahead, had fallen to his knees, staring down at something that lay behind Aaron Kingsley's tomb.

"No-o-o-o!" A great voice poured out of him, so primeval, so tortured, it ran an icy hand down Philip's spine.

"Brock, what is it?" Philip almost collapsed in shock, but recovered himself, stumbling to his cousin's side, though Brock turned his head to cry out a warning.

They both instinctively knew whose skeleton it was. And they both knew who had put the perfectly round hole in the skeleton's skull.

Philip, his face a mask of horror, turned and ran, barely making it outside before he began to retch his heart out.

How evil was the man he'd called Grandfather?

Inside the mausoleum Brock, his eyes closed, began to offer up the prayers he'd withheld for half his lifetime. This was his father, who'd once been young and handsome and strong. He had to hold onto his memories. He was at once a boy again, with tears sliding from beneath his lids. His father hadn't deserted them. He'd been here all along.

Spine-chilling horror turned to tremendous anxiety. "What are we going to do about this?" Philip, ashen-faced, looked apprehensively towards the house. "It's your father. It must be."

"It couldn't be anyone else," Brock responded, pressing both hands to his throbbing temples. "Even if he hadn't been wearing that medal around his neck I'd have known. My mother made him wear that to protect him." He gave a laugh so grim Philip shuddered. "Damn him to hell!"

They both knew who "him" was.

The cousins were sitting, in shock, on the stone steps that led up to the mausoleum, the great doors now firmly shut.

"I can't find the words to express how sorry I am, Brock." Philip shook his head in despair. "So very sorry.

There's no way any of us can make it up to you. We simply have to live with it. As a family, we're cursed."

"It seems like it," Brock answered in a blighted voice.

"What's going to happen when we make this public?" Philip asked, his voice terribly disturbed. "I can't bear to tell my mother. I don't even trust her. I'd hate Maitland to know. This will do frightful things to our family. To our name."

"Some family." Brock tried to focus his mind on all the consequences of their grim discovery. "Give me time to think this out. Kingsley is dead. The law can't touch him. But one thing I'll make clear. You're not going to put him in the mausoleum. That really would be a desecration. You'll tell your mother you've decided against it."

"Anything you say, Brock. I'll do whatever you want. I don't want him there with my poor father."

"You won't share this with anyone?"

"God, no." Philip shuddered all over. "Why would I want to? This is evil. I don't want Mulgaree either," he cried emotionally. "You can have it. I'm not simply making noises. You can have it. I'll sign it all over."

"I don't want it," Brock said in a flat, toneless voice. "I'd like to burn the bloody place down."

"And I'll help you. We can sell up. The whole shebang. You can handle it. You're much smarter than I am. Always were, always will be. As far as I'm concerned we can split the proceeds down the middle. This is the most sickening thing a man could expect to see in a lifetime outside of war. Grandfather must have thought he was God. Why did he do it? It's unbelievable."

Brock saw it with perfect clarity. "Jealousy. A jealousy that ate him away. Kingsley only had room in his heart for one person and that was my mother. When she betrayed him by marrying my father against his wishes that sealed my father's fate. It only took a few years for Kingsley to cross the line."

"How appalling!" said Philip, feeling as if he was on the

brink of bawling his eyes out. "I don't know if I've got
legs after this, but I have to put a stop to tomorrow's service.
To what I intended to happen. Forgive me, Brock, I know
this is sensitive but what will we do with your father's remains?"

"He must be properly buried." Probably in secret. Brock
wanted time to think.

"My dad too. Why don't we have this dreadful pile
knocked down?" Philip rose shakily to his feet. "Everyone
hates it."

"If I had my way I'd do it now. But first we have to
make arrangements. As for Kingsley? I've just decided. He
can be cremated. Send him away. Cancel the service. I don't
want him on this land."

"What are you saying, Philip? There's not to be a service
now?" Frances Kingsley, seated in an armchair, glared at
her son in astonishment.

"Brock and I have thought about it and we've decided
Grandfather will be cremated. We'll send him away."

Frances was clearly staggered. "Since when have you and
Brock been in agreement about anything?"

"Let it be, Frances," Brock said in a voice that carried
a lot of authority. "Arrangements have already been made.
We don't want him buried on Mulgaree."

"But it's his home. Was his home," Frances said, trying
to mute her own terrible memories of her father-in-law. "I
can't make sense of this at all. I never approved of the
mausoleum, as you well know. Dreadful place. In any case,
it's for Philip to decide, Brock. Philip is the heir."

"You have to prove the will first." Brock directed a glit-
tering glance at her. "I have far too many suspicions. Eula
is quite clear on one point. She saw Kingsley's signature.
Wait, Frances." He held up his hand as Frances made to
rush into denials. "Eula's not stupid. It's your way to seriously underestimate people. She was brought in as a wit-

ness and witness his signature she did. She will swear it on oath.''

"I don't want it anyway," Philip announced, still looking sick and ashen. "I'm not cut out for the top job. You know that, Mother. All I want is Shelley. If I have Shelley I don't need anything else."

"Except she's madly in love with your cousin, you fool," Frances cried, her face ugly with frustration and accumulated disappointment in her son.

Philip swung his head, an odd, defeated look on his face. "That's not true—is it, Brock?"

"Why don't you ask her?" Brock answered crisply.

"You see?" Anger coloured Frances's face. "I warned you. He's taken your girl."

"I think I want to hear that from Shelley herself," Philip said, sounding very subdued.

"You will," Brock promised. "Meanwhile, Frances, you can tell your boyfriend to pack his bags. I suspect the two of you are going to need a damned good lawyer."

Shelley had barely arrived back on Wybourne, her decision to leave her family firmly in her mind, when Brock called ahead to notify her he was arriving.

Patrick Logan looked threatened. "What's he coming here for? You'd better explain. It should be Philip."

Shelley shook her head. "Dad, you have to stop pushing Philip on me. It's all over. He may have been your choice, but never mine. I'm tired of trying to do things to make you happy. I've been trying all my life, but nothing works."

Her father towered above her. "All your mother and I want for you is your happiness, Shelley. I thought you went into town to think things over. Recover yourself."

"I did. That's why I'm making it as plain as I can. I have no romantic interest in Philip. I've been sympathetic towards him because of the way his grandfather treated him. It's Brock who means more to me." She could have said "everything to me", but that would have further inflamed her father.

Patrick Logan wheeled away, laughing as though she'd made some ridiculous jest. "I'm sorry, but what can *he* do for you? I understand he didn't get a penny."

"You insult me, Dad," Shelley answered with dignity. "I'm not interested in the money."

"No, because you're a silly little romantic fool," he retorted sharply. "You've got the ball in your hands but you're going to drop it. As far as I can recall, Brock Tyson had all the girls in love with him. Why do you suppose he's serious about you? And even if he were he can't help you. In all probability he's like his father. Ever think of that? Tyson abandoned his wife and child."

"Or rather his father went missing," Shelley said. "Rex Kingsley was a monstrous man. I'm sure he got to Brock's father in some way we'll never know." She turned her head, listening with the greatest relief to the sound of an approaching helicopter. "That will be Brock."

"And what do you propose to do?" her father challenged, weighed down by all sorts of guilt about himself but unable to confront them.

"Whatever he asks," Shelley said simply, walking to the door.

"You stay here, miss," her father roared. "I haven't lost the right to tell you what to do. This is my house, and while you're in it you'll do what you're told."

The tilt of her chin, the expression on her face, silenced him. "I'm terribly sorry, Dad, but I have been doing a lot of thinking. There's nothing for me here and there never really was. I'll pack my bags and make another life. I could tell you what happened that terrible day we lost Sean but it would only do more harm. I've remembered, you see. You'll be a lot happier when I'm gone. You never quite brought yourself to look at me."

"Come back here, Shelley." He gritted his teeth, trying

to speak more kindly. "I'll have a word with this young man."

"Don't expect him to be a push-over, like Philip," Shelley warned.

The meeting didn't go well. Brock was in no fit state to be sympathetic towards this man who had caused Shelley so much grief. Though he was courteous, just barely, hostility showed in his remarkable eyes.

Patrick Logan for his part found it an unexpectedly chastening experience. Though this young man's high-handed arrogance angered him, he found it oddly daunting. One thing was certain. Brock Tyson was no deserter. Probably the father hadn't been either. A man like Rex Kingsley was capable of anything after all—even blood on his hands.

Shelley's shock was immense when Brock told her the real story behind his father's disappearance. She watched him in alarm. Brock looked dangerous. "What are you going to do?" They had landed within Mulgaree's borders, a few miles from the homestead. "You want revenge?"

"Wouldn't you?" he asked tautly.

"I'm waiting for my heart to quiet," she said simply. "There must be terrible pain inside you."

For a minute he couldn't speak, traumatized, but trying to overcome it. "Pain and horror—yet in some way it's lifted a burden from my shoulders. I now know that my father didn't desert us. He must have faced up to Kingsley and suffered the terrible consequences. He may have said he was taking my mother and me away. That could have triggered a crime of passion. Sheer rage. My grandfather had a fearful temper. He'd hated my father from the start."

"Only you and Philip know?" She studied his grim profile.

"And now you. You need to know everything about me.

The good and the bad. There's an awful voice inside my head that reminds me I have Kingsley's blood.''

"Don't let that tear you apart, Brock. You're two completely different people. I would trust you with my life. I don't question your capacity to love or your compassion. Your grandfather sold his soul to the devil.''

"Let's hope the devil has got him now,'' Brock burst out violently.

Shelley sought to calm him, laying a hand on his arm. "Well, he's out of the picture for ever. He won't bother you any more. You can bring his crime to light or you can remain silent.''

"In silence I'd be protecting my family now and the family I hope to have one day. Would anyone want to know their great-grandfather had committed such a crime? I'll never forget it,'' Brock said sombrely. "Neither will Philip. It will haunt us to our dying day. So Kingsley gets off scot-free. Is that it?''

"Not when he meets his Maker,'' Shelley said with a shudder. "There is a Judgement Day, I'm sure of it. And in a way your grandfather was so miserable he answered all his life.''

Brock stared away to the purple ridges, a haze like gold dust hanging over their ragged peaks. "Philip tells me he wants to give up Mulgaree. It's the shock talking, of course.''

"I think I would too.'' She felt unnerved by the terrible disclosure.

Brock shook his head. "Mulgaree is the land. The land is eternal. We're only custodians. It's hard to think straight when you have to contend with so many dreadful things.''

"Finding your father like that must have been unbearable. I wish I'd been with you.'' They were sitting beneath a tree, she resting her head against his shoulder, desperate to offer comfort.

"You're here now.'' Brock's voice was deep and full of gratitude.

It moved Shelley immensely. "Don't I only complicate the picture?" she made herself ask.

"Shelley, there are complications all around," he groaned. "But you're keeping me sane. In fact, I'm damned sure I don't deserve you. I have problems to surmount before we can take up our lives. Right at this minute I'm not exactly sure what course to take. I have a strong case, but litigation costs a fortune—which is what Frances and Philip are banking on."

"I'll stand by you if you want me," she said, thinking of her promised reward for her part in finding the Claydon Treasure. She didn't know then, but it was far more than she'd ever expected. "As a friend," she said pointedly. "I would never want you to feel you had any obligation to me. That I couldn't live without you. That I'd jump off a cliff if you found another girl."

"Would you?" For the first time he smiled, an illumination that lit the handsome, sombre cast of his face.

"No."

"What would you do?" he asked very softly, lowering his head over hers, his lips at her temple.

"I'd sink into a terrible decline, but I'd go away and you wouldn't know a thing about it."

"Where would you go that I wouldn't find you?" His brilliant gaze challenged.

"Always supposing when things settle you'll want to find me?"

"You're talking nonsense, you know," he said, very crisply.

"Am I?" She knew what they had was good, but could she hold onto him?

"I'd hoped you'd know that by now," he told her in a taut voice.

Suddenly there were streaks of tears on her face.

"Shelley, am I being cruel to you?" He pulled her swiftly into his arms. "I don't mean to be. Nothing matters more than you."

"You want me to believe that?" She looked full into his beautiful eyes.

"Let me show you how much you matter," he said, and by way of answer laid her down on the sand.

One minute Eula was sitting at the kitchen table quietly shedding a few tears—her ladyship had given her notice, call it the sack, as of course she'd known she would, reminding Eula she had received a generous legacy to keep her comfortable if she was careful—when the largest part of her brain suddenly fired, emitting a chink of miraculous light.

She hadn't hidden the will in the Chinese vase. It was in the red lacquer Chinese chest with all the gold whirlygigs on it. There was so much Chinese stuff around the house— screens, rugs, chairs, chests, bronzes, vases almost as tall as her—you'd think you were in Beijing. The red lacquer chest—of course. It seemed incredible to her now that she hadn't been able to recall her hiding place despite all her efforts. What a great mysterious power the brain was. With any luck at all she'd be able to remember where she'd hidden her mother's gold brooch next.

Eula leapt up from her chair, feeling a great rush of hope. If anyone deserved to be compensated for all he and his lovely mother Catherine had suffered, it was Brock. That wicked old man owed him. Eula happened to know how much Brockway money had helped forge the Kingsley empire. A lot of people said money didn't matter. Eula thought it did.

The moment Brock and Shelley walked in the front door of the homestead, a great stillness about them, Eula hurried to give them the good news. Had she known it, triumph was emblazoned all over her face, her arms raised aloft in thanksgiving, her expression near ecstatic.

How happy it would make them, Eula thought, ignorant,

as she would remain, of Brock's tragic discovery. She wasn't sorry at all she had snatched up Maitland's handwritten document and copied it on the fax machine. She would swear that God had told her to do it.

Even so she had been amazed when she read it. Brock had been named the sole heir. There was no mention of anyone else. No bequests to the usual institutions—family, friends, servants. Including her. That blew her legacy, but she didn't care. Brock would never sack her. Of that she was certain.

What an extraordinary, unpredictable old man. Or maybe by the end he'd had no strength left but to make his will short and sweet. Brock had been the victim of his cruelty. Knowing Brock as well as she did, Eula was certain Brock would do the right thing by his cousin, Philip, but she sincerely hoped her ladyship wouldn't get a dime. She was an awful woman. Just awful.

Brock gave the housekeeper a piercing stare. "What is it, Eula?" God, the worst thing to do was to jump to conclusions.

Eula stumbled a little in her excitement to get to him. "I found it, Brock."

Brock reached down and grasped Shelley's hand, feeling as if his nerves were rubbed raw. "And?"

"I was just so happy that before I knew where I was I'd read it," Eula confessed, tossing Shelley a happy smile. "You get the lot. The whole shebang!"

Brock and Shelley stared at her as though they were trying hard to understand what she was saying. "What about Philip and his mother?" Brock questioned, his voice a little harsh, a pallor to his tanned polished skin.

"There's no mention of them!" Eula whispered from behind her hand.

Brock waited no more. "I've got to see this," he said, striding down the entrance hall, pulling Shelley with him, needing her, wanting her, releasing his feelings through the strong pressure of his hand. "Okay, so where is it?"

"It's just as I told you, Brock." Eula hurried after them, slightly out of puff. "Don't worry. It's in the kitchen. I wasn't going to let it out of my sight."

"So who do you love?" Brock suddenly demanded, halting to stare into Shelley's surprised emerald eyes.

She lifted her face to him, a dawning radiance chasing all the dark clouds away. She had a sudden mental image of herself as a bride, and knew happiness, a sense of belonging unrivalled in all the world.

"Do you love me?" he urged, seeing she was too overcome by emotion to speak. "Go on—say it, Shelley. I love you, Brock Tyson, even if you are a very difficult man. I love you and I want to spend the rest of my days with you. Swear it, Shelley. Suddenly the thought of losing you terrifies me."

He sounded in deadly earnest, his expression taut, his eyes like diamonds.

Very gently she reached up on tiptoe, locking her arms around his neck. "Brock Tyson, you fill me with wonder." Her voice communicated a deep loving intensity. "Love, what a miracle! I can't believe I've found it. Of course I love you. I was born to love you. I'll love you until I draw my last breath."

"And through eternity!" Brock slipped his arms around her, answering with corresponding emotion. As he gazed down at her a great hush grew between them, a full awareness of their commitment to each other. The great wisdom of it.

"Go on, kiss her!" Eula finally burst out, a beaming smile on her face. Picture it, picture it—these two lovely young people coming together! It was wonderful, and didn't they both deserve some happiness in life? "Bless me heart, Brock," she chortled. "You oughtta kiss her. Come on now, a big kiss."

"Thank you for that, Eula." Brock threw her a devastating smile that pinked her cheeks. Then, spreading his long fingers along Shelley's soft cheek, he bent his head and very thoroughly obliged.

This love of mine! he thought, filled with tenderness and desire. So precious. How had he got through life without loving Shelley? From this day forth there were new worlds to conquer. The prospect was tremendously exciting. He knew he could accomplish anything with Shelley by his side.

EPILOGUE

Mulgaree Station, four months later

ACROSS the huge bedroom Shelley caught her reflection in the free-standing cheval mirror. She looked beautiful, more beautiful than she had ever hoped to look in her life. Her wedding dress was gold-tinged ivory silk, with a strapless bodice hand-sewn with exquisite crystals, tiny pearls and beads. The skirt, tightly waisted, was similarly decorated, billowing in a wonderfully romantic fashion to the floor.

She wore a three-quarter veil, the tulle bordered for some inches in the same ivory-gold shot silk as her gown, held in place by a diadem of roses fashioned from ivory and gold silk. It curved around her head, the colour and lustre accenting the red-gold of her hair, which she'd left flowing because that was the way Brock liked it. That he loved her so deeply she still found astonishing. Brock was her future, her dream, her heart.

Around her neck and in her ears she wore his gift to her.

"With your skin, it just has to be pearls," he'd told her, bending to kiss her cheeks, her mouth, her throat.

And what pearls they were! The finest in the world. They had flown to Broome in the Northern Territory, the headquarters of the Australian pearling industry, to select them. They were perfectly matched, their lustre unique.

"I want nothing less for my bride!" Brock had declared proudly.

Today she and Brock were drawing a line between their past life and their future. The past, with all its traumas, pain and uncertainties, had found closure. Their future they faced together. Happiness in place of grief.

She had two bridesmaids. One was her childhood friend, Nicole Cavanagh, a redhead like herself, but so much more beautiful, Shelley privately thought. Nicole had recently returned to her illustrious family home, Mara Station, after several years abroad, living and working in Paris and New York. Nicole had her own dramatic story to tell. Traumas she hadn't yet said goodbye to. Shelley realized with a feeling of accomplishment that Nicole had gained comfort from renewing their friendship over the last few weeks.

Her other bridesmaid was her sister, Amanda. Shutting Amanda and the family out of her big day would have been more than she could deal with.

Philip was Brock's groomsman. His best man was Drake McClelland. A name to contend with. It had bothered Shelley immensely at the beginning, bringing Nicole and Drake together in the bridal party, but Brock had convinced her it might be a good thing. The Cavanaghs and the McClellands, once the greatest friends, had been turned into mortal enemies for over a decade because of one terrible event that had destroyed the relationship. Shelley didn't want to dwell on it on this day of days, when happiness reigned.

Brock might have banished Philip's mother from Mulgaree for ever, but these past hectic months had forged a bond between the cousins. They had reached a private agreement whereby Philip had a substantial stake in Kingsley Holdings with Brock holding the reins. Philip, with the help of an excellent overseer, now lived and worked on Strathdownie Station, a central link in the chain. These days he was a different man. He'd been able to move on, though Shelley suspected he would always have a soft spot for her.

Although he had been in the ideal position to, Brock had not pressed charges against Philip's mother and her lover Gerald Maitland. Not a decision taken easily or lightly, it had all been designed to protect the family. Frances had received an allowance from her son and a dire warning to stay away; Gerald Maitland had been made to retire from his prestigious firm, citing a need to "wind down". The decree was absolute. Both obeyed. In many families some things were kept secret. Nevertheless, private justice had to be served.

In preparation for the wedding Mulgaree homestead had been transformed. A small army of decorators had been brought in, working closely with Shelley who had carried with her innumerable sketches to influence the designers. In a way it had been like realizing a dream, especially when the team had taken her creativity seriously. There wasn't one fabric or wall-covering she hadn't picked.

"We could give you a job any time!" she had been told constantly, and this was not flattery but genuine admiration.

Her job, her life's work, was to become Brock's perfect partner. Wife, mother, best friend. She always consulted him, but he was kept very busy indeed with Kingsley affairs.

"I want what you want. It's that simple," he'd told her. "I couldn't say that to too many people," he'd added dryly, hugging her to his side. Indeed, he had been very critical of the gloomy old mansion, asking that light and fresh air should be brought in.

And from the old Kingsley mansion a new house had been born.

At precisely three p.m., as the lovely processional music began in the grand formal drawing room, Shelley put her hand over her father's. Today he looked so much better than he had looked in a very long time, and even her mother's face was soft and pretty with pleasure. Since she'd woken up Shelley had had a sensation of being very close to her twin, Sean. In her heart she knew he would always be there.

Her father's hand tightened on hers. Strong hands. There were no whispered words. No talk of love. No plea for forgiveness. But still he tried to communicate through his hand. She would have to accept this as enough.

They paused on the threshhold.

Everything came into vivid focus.

Up ahead was her wonderful bridegroom with his attendants. All of them six footers plus. All of them cattlemen from family dynasties. Pioneers of the industry and descendants of some of the first settlers to open up the vast Outback. They were standing in front of great banks of beautiful, fragrant white flowers—orchids, lilies, roses, clouds and clouds of white baby's breath.

Each step would take Shelley closer to Brock. She knew from the set of his tall lean body, so marvellously elegant in his wedding finery, that he was struggling not to turn round and look back at her.

A smile bloomed radiantly across Shelley's face. A wonderful light lit her eyes.

Let life begin! She was ready for the challenge.

* * * * *

Read on for an extract from Nicole's story.
Coming soon in

Koomera Crossing

from
Margaret Way

CHAPTER ONE

GOD knows what made him turn back to look around the airport terminal. And at that precise moment. Otherwise he'd have missed her. For a moment he stood immobilized by shock, feeling as if a hand had reached in and twisted his heart.

Nicole Cavanagh.

Too much history! But the powerful physical attraction was still there.

She had her back to him, standing at the conveyor belt waiting for her luggage. He'd have recognised her by her hair alone. It was difficult to describe that glorious colour, but it always made him think of rubies. Today the familiar cascade of long curling hair was pulled into an elegant knot.

As she turned a young woman, over-zealous to collect her luggage, surged forward, nearly crashed into her—he could see that flawless skin, milk-white with fatigue, large, faintly slanted blue-green eyes even at that distance shadowed lilac with exhaustion.

Not that anything could dim her beauty or the aura she gave off. Every woman he met fell short of Nicole. She was wearing a sleeveless top, high-necked, in a shimmery golden-beige, narrow black trousers, high-heeled sandals, and a wide tan leather belt with an ornate gold buckle rested on her hips. She looked what she was. A thoroughbred. High-stepping, classy, on the nervy side. Why wouldn't she be, after what she'd been through?

No matter their dark history, he found it impossible to quietly disappear. Simply go on his way and ignore her. He'd heard Heath Cavanagh was back on Mara. Obviously she'd returned home to assess the situation. The character of the man who had estranged father and daughter.

"Wait for me, could you?" he asked Dawkins who, as an employee of an employee, was obliged to do whatever he wanted anyway. "I've just spotted a friend."

"Right, sir."

A friend? he asked himself, feeling all his nerves tighten. More like a veiled enemy. Nevertheless, he made for the conveyor belt.

Forrester Square

LEGACIES . LIES . LOVE .

Award-winning author Day Leclaire
brings a highly emotional and
exciting reunion romance story to
Forrester Square in December...

KEEPING FAITH

by

Day Leclaire

Faith Marshall's dream of a "white-picket" life with
Ethan Dunn disappeared—along with her husband—
when she discovered that he was really a dangerous
mercenary. With Ethan missing in action, Faith found
herself alone, pregnant and struggling to survive.
Now, years later, Ethan turns up alive. Will a family
reunion be possible after so much deception?

Forrester Square...
Legacies. Lies. Love.

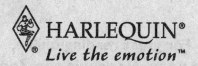

HARLEQUIN®
Live the emotion™

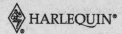
HARLEQUIN®

INTRIGUE®

Nestled deep in the Cascade Mountains of Oregon, the close-knit community of Timber Falls is visited by evil. Could one of their own be lurking in the shadows...?

CASCADES CONCEALED

B.J. Daniels

takes you on a journey to the remote Northwest in a new series of books far removed from the fancy big city. Here, folks are down-to-earth, but some have a tendency toward trouble when the rainy season comes...and it's about to start pouring!

Look for

MOUNTAIN SHERIFF
December 2003

and

DAY OF RECKONING
March 2004

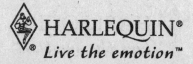
HARLEQUIN®
Live the emotion™

Visit us at www.eHarlequin.com

HICQMS

The world's bestselling romance series.

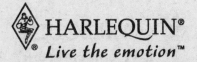

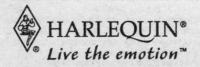